Her Dreamy Deceiver

The Worthington Legacy
Book Two

Marie Higgins

Dearest Reader;

Thank you for your support of a small press. At Dragonblade Publishing, we strive to bring you the highest quality Historical Romance from some of the best authors in the business. Without your support, there is no 'us', so we sincerely hope you adore these stories and find some new favorite authors along the way.

Happy Reading!

CEO, Dragonblade Publishing

Additional Dragonblade books by Author Marie Higgins

The Worthington Legacy
Her Perfect Scoundrel (Book 1)
Her Dreamy Deceiver (Book 2)

Love's Addiction Series
A Wallflower to Love (Book 1)
A Governess to Protect (Book 2)
A Maiden to Remember (Book 3)

The Earl of Hanover, Collin Worthington, runs across the woman he had wanted over a year ago, but she married his friend. While trying to repair the damage made to Cassandra Talbot, he finds himself trapped in his feelings again. Will she ever forgive him?

Lady Cassandra Kentwood was forced to marry the wrong man, and now all she wants is revenge. But when Collin is injured and she takes care of him, she remembers the reason she fell in love with him in the first place. But she doesn't want those feelings any longer.

Chapter One

Leicestershire, England

T O ERR IS *human, to forgive divine,* Alexander Pope once said. But for Cassandra, the man who had *erred* against her had started a whirlwind of tragic mistakes, pulling her deeper and deeper into misery. Although she wanted to forgive, now was not the time, and she couldn't see it in her future.

Righting the wrong was the only way for her to finally leave the horrid past behind her so that she could get on with her life.

Cassandra Talbot, Marchioness of Kentwood, bounced on the seat of the coach as the driver took her to Hanover Hall in Leicestershire. Today was Lord William Worthington's wedding, a function that Cassandra had not been invited to attend. It made little difference. She wasn't going to the manor to see Lord William anyway. It was his older brother, the Earl of Hanover, that she planned to ruin.

Shaking her head, she shifted on the seat and peered out the window. Perhaps *ruin* wasn't the appropriate word. After all, she would never be able to ruin Collin Worthington's life, since he was a titled lord with a powerful family standing behind him. However, she could make Collin a laughingstock in front of his friends, and especially all the maidens attending the wedding in hopes of becoming the lord's wife.

Cassandra figured she was doing those women a service by making certain their hearts did not get broken, and their lives wrecked.

She lightly tapped her fingers on the window of the coach, wishing everything could be over by now. Being anxious like this was wearing on her nerves.

For a little over a year, she had been planning today's event with great anticipation. It would happen the way *she* wanted because it was time that something right happened in her life. She would march into that wedding party, make herself known, and everyone would hear what she had to say about the so-called nobleman. Then, after seeing Collin's shocked and very humiliated expression, she would leave quickly and never look back.

And she would *not* feel guilty. After all, why should she? She had never believed in revenge—until she met him. Now, that was all she thought about.

Collin Worthington was the first and only man she had ever met who went out of his way to charm her. He hadn't judged or found her wanting because of her family's impoverished circumstances. It was impossible for her not to be affected by his actions. Indeed, he had made it very easy for her to surrender her heart to him.

He had also inherited her deceased husband's title.

She clenched her teeth as her stomach rolled. That particular event she could have done without, because now Collin was the one who owned her lands and her home. If he wanted, he could toss her out without a shilling to her name. Sadly, she didn't care about money, since all she wanted was to be free of her thoughts and anger.

This was yet another ideal reason to make him upset with her. Just because he held the title of Marquess of Kentwood now, that didn't mean she had to tiptoe around him. Indeed, she would speak her mind. She didn't care if he took her residence, although he had so many estates already that she wondered if he would want hers. Nevertheless, she would find other lodging, even if she had to move in with one of her brothers.

The rocking motion of her traveling coach slowed, and she concentrated on the landscape from the window as Hanover Hall grew nearer. Her stomach twisted and she willed the uncomfortable feelings to stop. Doubts snuck into her mind, but she pushed them aside. *I am doing the right thing!*

Grumbling, Cassandra shook her head. She must believe this was the only way to right a wrong. Never in her life had she been so determined to make another person miserable. She had always been kind and forgiving, but he had turned her into a vicious woman. But then, never before had she been put in a scandalous situation and had to sit and watch someone control her life. Before, she couldn't do anything. But now, she was in control.

The coach came to a full stop, and she took in a deep breath, repeating in her mind that she could do this. She had worn one of her favorite gowns that she had specifically made as Lloyd Talbot's wife, only because it was expensive. She wanted to flaunt it in front of him, just to see his expression when she told him the cost, but sadly, that day had never happened. He had died two days later when he and his drinking friends were in a boat that capsized—killing only her husband.

She ran her palm over the blue and silver satin material. This particular style of gown was all the rage in Paris, so the seamstress had told her. Madame Fowler had mentioned that women were wearing gowns with fuller sleeves and lower waistlines. Cassandra actually liked the full sleeves, and the lower waistline really made her look slimmer.

Quickly removing her cloak, she scooted to the edge of the seat, waiting for the footman to open the door. He reached a hand inside, she took it, and he helped her down. She squared her shoulders and walked away from the vehicle with her head held high like a true marchioness, even though she had never truly felt like one.

She scanned the crowded yard but didn't recognize anyone yet. That was a good thing. She didn't want anyone to stop her before she accomplished her task. But it didn't matter. Even if someone tried to stop her, she would push them aside and continue on her way. She wouldn't leave until Collin was humiliated.

Then she saw him, and for a moment, her heartbeat stalled. Collin Worthington stood with his back toward her, but she would recognize the tall, broad-shouldered man with the wheat-blond hair anywhere. Standing in his little circle was an older man and three young ladies. The women stared up at the tall, broad-shouldered marquess with dreams in their eyes. Cassandra would make certain she squashed their hopes. The newly appointed Marquess of Kentwood was not the marrying kind. The rogue was far from being a true gentleman.

Memories she had wanted to keep hidden tried to resurface. She mustn't remember how he made her heart skip with excitement when he first smiled at her, or how he left her weak in the knees just from his passionate kisses. Instead, she must remind herself just how much she hated him for allowing his friend to take his place at the cottage when she thought she was secretly meeting Collin.

She walked through the wedding crowd to where Collin would easily notice her. People glanced her way as she headed toward the marquess, but her focus was only on him. Finally, his head turned toward her. For a second, his gaze swept briefly over her, but when he finally studied her face, his eyes widened. She wasn't prepared for the excitement that flashed across his expression, but she wouldn't let that sway her determination.

He wasn't excited to see her. He probably wanted to give her his sympathies for the passing of the rotten man she married. Then again, she expected him to schedule a time to talk to her about the estate and how he was now in charge.

Collin mumbled something to those around him even though his gaze never left her. Then he headed her way. She should have stopped and let him come to her, but she still worried someone would try to converse with her. The only reason she had come was for him, so her steps didn't slow.

When they reached each other, they stopped. His gaze roamed over her face as if he were trying to memorize her. She remembered him doing that a few times before when they had been together. Her heartbeat quickened and she clenched her jaw, praying she could do everything she had planned.

"Cass," he whispered, the nickname he had given her, almost in reverence. "What...are you doing here?"

The ice she had purposely built around her heart began to melt. Quickly, before it completed its task, she remembered how he had ruined her life. She would *not* allow him to weaken her ever again.

She swallowed hard before clearing her throat. "I couldn't go another day without seeing you. So much has been on my mind since we last talked, and I needed to tell you about my feelings before any more time passes."

Confusion creased his forehead, and he looked behind her briefly. "You have been thinking of me?"

Slowly, she breathed, trying to gain control again. "I don't know how to answer that."

"Why not?"

"Because I have been thinking of you, but not the way you probably imagine."

He hitched a breath. "But...you *have* thought of me."

She tried to breathe calmly, even though her heartbeat raced. Seeing the sparkle in his hazel eyes wasn't a good thing. "How could I not? You are the one who inherited my dead husband's title."

The light that had been in his eyes dimmed. "Cass, believe me when I say I'm truly sorry for your loss." He paused briefly. "What happened, if you don't mind my asking?"

She frowned. "You don't know?"

"The first I had heard of this was a couple of weeks ago."

Slowly, she shook her head. "He has been dead for a year now. He died two days after we were married."

Collin gasped and lifted his hand to his lips. His rapid blinking made her wonder if he was trying to hold back tears. And yet the expression that flitted across his face showed he was vastly relieved but felt guilty about it. Still, she couldn't allow that to sway her from her goal.

"Forgive me," he said in a whisper, "but can you tell me how…how did he die?"

"He and a few of his cronies went out on a boat that capsized. My intoxicated husband was the only one who drowned." Cassandra didn't dare mention that strumpets had been on the boat with those men. Knowing her husband had been unfaithful so soon after they exchanged vows was quite humiliating and not something she shared with anyone.

"I'm…so sorry, Cassandra. I honestly didn't know."

She arched an eyebrow. "*You* are sorry?"

"Of course. Talbot had been my very good friend at one time. I'm sure you were devastated to have your husband die so quickly after the wedding."

She rolled her eyes. "For your information, my lord, I was *not* devastated. If you recall, our marriage was one that neither Lord Kentwood nor I had wanted."

Collin frowned. "Yes, I remember." His hand dropped to his side, and he squared his shoulders. "So, tell me, what are you doing at my brother's wedding? Did you want to discuss the manors and which one you will receive?"

As she fought the feelings of doubt about her reactions, she focused on all the pain and agony she had experienced since meeting him. Tears stung her eyes, but she would not shed them. Collin Worthington wasn't worth the effort. Not any longer.

"That is not why I'm here." She took a reassuring breath. "I sought you out today to tell you how much I despise you."

His eyes widened once again. "Pardon me?"

"Because of what happened just more than a year ago…you ruined me. I have been utterly miserable, and it's all your fault."

His brows drew together. "I ruined you? How do you figure

that when Talbot was the one who—"

"Because," she quickly interrupted him, "you did *nothing* to stop it or even prevent it from happening."

Collin sighed heavily and pushed his fingers through his wavy hair. "I fear you're not making any sense. How could I have possibly stopped it?"

Anger grew inside of her, and she fisted her hands. "Because," she said through tight lips, "you did not come to the cottage like you told me you would."

"The cottage?" He shook his head.

Cassandra had had enough of this guessing game. He played the innocent, and not very well. Before he said something to soften her heart, it was time to make others see him for the fool she knew him to be.

She released a very loud, agitated sigh. "You *ruined* my family with your roguish actions," she shouted. "You ruined...my life, and I shall never forgive you for that."

Gradually, the wedding crowd became quiet, which was exactly what she wanted. Collin stood frozen, and his face had lost a little color. His throat jumped in what must have been a hard swallow.

"Cass—"

"I'm *Lady* Kentwood to you!"

Collin grasped her arm, but she yanked it away and stepped back.

"I think," he said calmly, "that we should take this conversation somewhere that is more private instead of airing our grievances in public."

"Private?" she shrieked. "So that you can ruin my reputation even more?"

He gave her a stern look. "Lady Kentwood, I really must insist—"

"You can insist all you like, for the good it will do. But I will never willingly go into a private room with you ever again."

Malice darkened Collin's eyes. She never thought she would

witness such anger in his expression, but it was worth every second. Victory was within reach. Revenge was such sweet medicine for her soul.

"Lady Kentwood," he grumbled for her ears only, "you are making a spectacle of yourself. If I didn't know you better, I would think that you have been drinking from your late husband's liquor cabinet."

She gave him an evil grin and shook her head. "No," she said softly, "I have never touched the stuff, and I never will. This outrage you see is all me. It has been inside me since I was forced to marry Lord Talbot."

Silence stretched between her and Collin, but moments later, two men joined them. One of the men resembled Collin, but his hair was a dark brown. Each man stood on opposite sides of her and firmly grasped an elbow. This was her cue to leave, which she would, since her work here was completed.

"I do not know who you are," the man who looked like Collin said in a gruff voice, "but you were not invited to my wedding, and so my cousin and I are going to escort you back to your coach."

Cassandra looked back at Collin, showing him through her glare just how much she loathed him. She didn't take her eyes off him even as the two men led her away from the wedding guests.

Finally, when they reached her coach, she pulled away from them. She rested her attention on the bridegroom. "I beg your forgiveness for ruining your party, but it was your brother whom I wanted to embarrass, not you."

The man lifted his chin. "Lady Kentwood, I think *you* are the one who has been embarrassed the most here today."

She shook her head, trying to keep her heart from breaking all over again. It was over now, so why didn't she feel satisfied? "No, I set out to humiliate the new Marquess of Kentwood. Now that I have had the last laugh, I will leave and never return."

With unshed tears stinging her eyes, she turned and climbed into her coach. When she sat on the seat, she sighed with relief as her body trembled. She had waited for a whole year to get that off her chest.

Why, then, did she feel like her world was crumbling around her all over again?

Chapter Two

COLLIN'S BODY AND mind felt like they had shut down, and all he could do was stare in the direction his brother and cousin had taken Cassandra. Although he tried to absorb all she had said, the words were jumbled in his head and made no sense. Of course, her making an appearance after all this time was a shock in itself. The last time he laid eyes on Cass was at a country dance in Bath. She had looked so lovely that night.

He had found himself staring at her intoxicating beauty quite often during the evening, wanting to lose himself in her amazing blue eyes. He had listened for her musical laugh, and his heart skipped a beat during those precious moments.

When she had agreed to dance with him those few times, he felt like a king in her presence, since he was with the loveliest woman he had ever seen. And when she chatted with him afterward, his desire for the enchanting woman grew. Somehow, in one evening, she had crawled into his heart and mind.

During their stroll outside in the night's shadows, he couldn't contain himself and just had to kiss her. Although he knew she was innocent, she had responded the way he'd hoped, which made his heart melt.

But what had happened to the sweet, innocent woman he once knew? It was obvious the last year had been unkind to her. There was so much anger in her expression that it made the sparkle disappear entirely from her pretty blue eyes.

When she was shouting at him only a few minutes ago, his first response had been to take away her pain. However, when she had turned vengeful, that was when he realized something wasn't right. Half of the accusations she threw at him were untrue. And yet she made such a commotion, she must believe they had happened. Cass wasn't the kind of woman to have such harsh feelings just because she wanted to hurt someone. There must be some underlying reason to her apparent madness.

His heart had broken a little when she told him about Lord Talbot's death, but Collin's sympathy ended in the face of her tirade. The more her words echoed in his head, the greater his anger became. He couldn't let her get away this time. Not without explaining a few things. Why did she blame him for ruining her life? Everything that happened in Bath had been her decision.

Without thinking about his actions, he broke into a run, moving in the direction his brother and cousin, Trey Worthington, had escorted her to her coach. As Collin rounded the bend, the vehicle was heading away from the manor. His brother and cousin stared at him with confused expressions. Trey appeared sorrowful, whereas Adrian looked downright angry by the disruption of his wedding.

"Collin," Adrian began, touching Collin's shoulder, "I'm truly sorry about—"

"I need to go after her," Collin snapped as he hurried toward a nearby horse.

"Have you gone insane?" Adrian's voice lifted as he chased after Collin. "She completely humiliated you in front of everyone. And you want to go after her?"

"You don't understand." Collin unhooked the reins from the post and effortlessly mounted. He pierced his younger brother with a scowl. "You don't know what happened between us. And I need to make things right."

He didn't listen for his brother's reply, and urged the horse toward the road heading away from the estate. He prayed he could catch up. Trying to find her if he lost her now would be quite troublesome, only because he had never been to Lord Talbot's small estate. However, he was certain someone would give him directions if he asked.

Leaning forward, he kicked the horse's belly, urging the animal faster. Hopefully, Adrian would locate the owner of the horse and apologize for Collin's taking the animal without asking. But right now, he only cared about one thing.

Up ahead, he spotted the coach, so he slowed the horse. He didn't want to alert her that he was following, and nor did he want to stop her coach just to talk. Instead, he would wait until she stopped wherever she was staying. He doubted she lived around here, but he was certain that she rented a room at an inn. Or perhaps she had relatives or friends who were in this area.

His thoughts shifted back to when he first met Cassandra, and he scrambled to remember the moment he could have been to blame for ruining her life. She married a wealthy marquess, so why had she acted as though she was forced? Most women Collin knew would have loved to have the life of a marchioness.

But most women weren't Cassandra.

He had discovered that about the woman the very day they met. Although he admitted to being judgmental at first, looking down on her because of her impoverished family, she had been nothing but kind...in her stubborn way. Soon, he realized his mistake in thinking so poorly of her, because she was the first woman to touch his heart.

Another hour passed quickly, and Collin continued to follow the coach at a distance. His thoughts were still jumbled, and he didn't know what to say to her when he finally got her alone. At least he wouldn't be as tongue-tied as he'd been at Adrian's wedding, but her surprise shocked him nearly speechless.

The weather turned cooler, and thick gray clouds filled the sky. The light wind from earlier today had picked up speed. A storm was brewing, he could feel it in his bones. Dust blew across the road, hindering his vision. He prayed the coach would reach its destination before the sky opened and dumped rain on him, since he had no heavy garment to protect him from the chill.

Finally, the fancy coach turned toward an estate—one he recognized. This had been Lloyd's first estate before the man inherited the marquess title. Lloyd hadn't liked being so far from civilization, and so he had purchased a larger estate closer to Birmingham. At first, he had considered the estate in Leicester-shire to be his country estate, but when his gaming and womanizing had become the center of his life, he stayed closer to Birmingham.

Frowning, Collin shook his head. He still couldn't believe his friend was dead. And to think, if Collin had stayed home instead of traveling the world, he would have known about Lloyd's accident…and about the widow's deep hatred toward him.

As he entered the estate grounds, he slowed his horse. He didn't want her to see him just yet. The element of surprise would be the best way to handle this, just as when she had stunned him into silence earlier today.

The coach stopped in front of the manor, and the footman jumped off the seat of the coach and hurried around to the vehicle's door. Collin guided the horse into a group of trees and brought the animal to a stop. Watching closely, he waited for Cassandra to exit the coach while the wind whipped around him, making him wish he had brought his thick, fur-lined cape.

Finally, the blue and silver of her gown captured his atten-tion. Her silky wheat-golden hair hung in ringlets, resting on her shoulders. She was as stunning now as she had been when he first saw her at the ball he and Lloyd had attended in Bath.

Sighing heavily, he frowned. How he wished he could return to that time when he first started falling in love with her. He would handle things completely differently. For one, he wouldn't have allowed Lloyd to marry her, even if it was the proper thing to do. Collin's heart had suffered all this time because he hadn't been more forthright with his feelings for her and stood up to his cousin.

The rustling of bushes from behind him pulled his focus away from Cassandra. Although the wind was blowing hard, the sound he heard wasn't from the storm that was nearly upon them. He glanced over his shoulder just in time to see a thick tree limb swinging toward his face. The object connected with his head in a loud thump. Pain lanced through him like a sharp knife, blocking his ears and making his vision unclear. He lost his grip on the reins and fell off the horse. His body hit the ground, but the pain in his head overrode anything else.

Cursing under his breath, Collin tried to rise to his feet, but he was having difficulty even kneeling. Through his dizzy vision, he saw the dark blue suit coat and matching breeches of the man who had hit him. Not only that, but Collin noticed a thinning bald spot on the back of his head. But he knew for a certainty that the man was a servant.

Releasing a shout of anger, Collin struggled against the pain and how darkness tried to take over his vision and mind, trying to jump on the imbecile, but the man was quicker. Collin's body succumbed to weakness. A warm, sticky substance slid down the side of his face where the limb had connected to his head. He didn't need to touch it to know that blood coated his skin and hair.

Panic welled inside him. A blow to the head could kill a man. He needed to stop the bleeding. Unfortunately, his weak body wouldn't cooperate with his mind as he tried to loosen his cravat in hopes of wrapping the garment around his head to control the flow of blood.

In a state of helplessness, he dropped back to the ground, his face turned to one side. Slowly, his vision faded while he watched his attacker run away. Darkness filled his eyes and he struggled to keep his eyes open. He prayed this was not the end of his life. There was so much that needed to be resolved, especially with Cassandra. He said a silent prayer that God would keep him alive.

CASSANDRA'S MIND WAS still in turmoil from her visit with Collin as she slowly climbed the porch steps heading up toward the two-story manor. Now that she had gotten her frustration for the way her life had turned out off her chest, she waited for the moment of peace. So why wasn't it happening yet? She had waited so long to feel the relief of confronting Collin about his wrongdoings that she wouldn't know what to do with her time now, since she planned on finally putting him out of her mind forever.

Suddenly, off in the distance, she heard a man's painful shout. She stopped and turned toward the coach. Both the driver and footman stood near the vehicle, peering toward the glade of trees on her property.

"What is going on?" she asked, lifting her voice above the howling wind.

"My lady," Bentley said, pointing in the direction of their gazes. "I just noticed a servant running away as if the devil nipped at his heels."

Cassandra had always been a curious woman, and today was no different. Of course, because she had heard someone in pain, she knew they must investigate.

She headed back down the steps and toward the group of trees. The driver and footman keeping up with her hurried pace. It didn't take long to see the gray material of the man's clothes, and his wheat-blond hair.

Her mind stumbled and she sucked in a breath. There was only one man who had hair like that, the only man whose memory popped into her head whenever she saw that color. But it couldn't be *him*.

Bentley and Riddle ran ahead of her, reaching the man lying still on the ground before she could. She slowed her steps until she recognized the wide shoulders and muscular body of the man she had wanted to forget.

"My lady," Bentley said, staring at her. "He has been seriously injured."

Standing frozen, she ran her gaze over Collin's unconscious body, but especially the blood pouring from his head and turning his hair red—and the tree limb near his body with spots of his blood.

"Is…he dead?" she asked hesitantly.

The footman shrugged. "I'm not certain, my lady." He glanced at the driver. "I do not know how to tell."

In his fortieth year, Bentley had been a reliable driver and trusted friend. His sour expression as he stared at the unconscious man lying on the ground gave Cassandra an uneasy feeling that she wasn't going to like the answer.

"Bentley, check to see if his chest is moving," she instructed him.

As the potbellied driver knelt beside Collin, a strong wind knocked against her, making her tilt slightly. She bundled the cape around her neck tighter and glanced at the sky. Dark clouds moved closer to them, thickening by the second. If they didn't get inside, they would be soaked clean through in a few minutes.

She shifted her attention back to Collin. Bentley had his ear on the unconscious man's chest. She held her breath, waiting for the outcome.

Seconds slipped by quickly, and she feared the worst. Whatever happened out here, someone had killed Collin. Although she should be happy that he was finally out of her life, her chest tightened. It didn't matter if he had broken her heart and ruined her—she did not wish him dead.

Suddenly, Bentley snapped to a sitting position and aimed his wide eyes on her.

"He is breathing, my lady."

Relief rushed through her as another strong wind threatened to unbalance her. "Bentley, Riddle, as carefully as you can, take the man inside the manor. I will have Dora make a room ready for him."

"But my lady," the footman said, gliding his palm over his slicked-back hair. "Who will care for him?" He glanced up at the darkening sky. "It might be too late to fetch a doctor."

"Nevertheless, we must help him, or he will die." She motioned toward Collin. "There is no time to waste."

As the servants lifted Collin, she turned and ran back toward the manor. The strong wind blew against her face now, making her movements slower than necessary. Indeed, with a storm like this, would she be able to send one of her servants to fetch a doctor? And would the doctor want to travel in such weather conditions?

She raised her gown to her calves and climbed the porch steps, taking two at a time. The door to the manor was already open as her housekeeper stood just inside, watching Cassandra with wide eyes.

"Dora, quickly," Cassandra ordered her, "get a room ready. Someone is injured and we must care for him."

The housekeeper nodded and darted toward the stairs, going as fast as her fifty-year-old body would take her. Cassandra yanked off her cloak as she hurried behind the woman. They entered the first guest room, and the housekeeper moved to the bed, pulling down the blankets. Cassandra went to the window and pulled open the curtains, adding more light to the room. She turned and took the lamp, igniting a flame.

"My lady?" Marybeth asked from the doorway.

Cassandra glanced over her shoulder at the maid. "What do you need?"

"Should I go fetch Doctor Hadley?"

Cassandra peered out the window again and groaned. The rain was already falling, but soon the roads would be impossible to travel on.

Sighing, she turned her attention to the young maid whose freckles took over most of her face. "I thank you for offering, but I fear the storm will keep the doctor from coming. It's best if we stay inside now. However, if you will find some bandages and have Tabitha bring up some warm water, that will be very helpful."

"Yes, my lady." Marybeth curtsied and darted down the corridor.

Cassandra knelt in front of the hearth and proceeded to start a fire. Behind her, Dora gasped.

"My lady! You should not be doing that."

Cassandra didn't look at the housekeeper. Instead, she rolled her eyes and continued to get a fire going. These servants must have forgotten that she hadn't been raised as a *real lady* and didn't go to finishing school to learn decorum. Growing up, she had learned to sew, cook, clean, and yes—even start a fire.

"We don't have time for someone else to do it," she told the housekeeper.

The older woman knelt beside Cassandra and set more kindling inside the hearth. "Then allow me to assist you."

Once the flames took over the kindling, men's boot steps echoed on the floor outside the room. Cassandra rose to her feet and helped the housekeeper stand. Cassandra's gaze fell to the woman's dirty bosom and arms.

Confused, she shook her head. "Dora? Why is your dress filthy?"

The woman's face flamed red. "Well, you see… I, um…" Her throat jumped in what must have been a hard swallow. "When I realized the storm was coming, I ran outside to cover the tomato bushes. We cannot have the rain destroying our lovely garden."

"Indeed. I do love tomatoes," Cassandra replied.

Within seconds, Bentley and Riddle carried in Collin and placed him on the bed. Thankfully, the men were not wet, which meant they had made it inside the manor before the sky opened with moisture.

Cassandra and Dora assisted in removing the injured man's clothes, but before Collin's trousers or shirt could be taken off, the housekeeper raised a hand, stopping everyone.

"Lady Kentwood," Dora began. "I realize you are widowed,

but it isn't proper to be in the room as we undress another man."

Inwardly, Cassandra groaned. Her housekeeper was correct, and being in here would only injure her reputation that much more. "Fine, I shall leave, but once you are finished, I need to return and bandage his head."

"Yes, my lady." Dora nodded and escorted Cassandra to the door.

Once Cassandra walked into the hall, the housekeeper closed the door. The pounding in Cassandra's head grew worse, and she rubbed her temples. This really couldn't be happening. Her luck had turned from bad to worse. What in the blazes was Collin Worthington doing at her estate? What had made him want to follow when she returned home after trying to humiliate him in front of his brother's wedding guests?

She hoped to get answers soon. The wait would surely drive her insane.

Chapter Three

GROWLING, CASSANDRA PACED the hall in front of the bedroom. Had Collin followed her back to the manor to apologize? Or had he just wanted to air his grievances about their past, since she hadn't really given him a chance to speak his mind? Either way, it might have gotten him killed.

She stopped and leaned against the railing, peering down the stairs to the manor's main level. Who could have possibly wanted to hurt him? Bentley said he saw a servant running away, yet she doubted her servants would have been so bold to strike a titled lord. In the year she had known them, she saw they were not even brave enough to face her irate husband, and they rarely spoke to her, since they knew she was from a lower class of people.

The ache in her head from these unknown questions moved her feet again as she resumed her pacing. If not for the storm, she would have sent riders out to fetch the doctor and the constable. Purposely causing harm to a noble was against the law and might get the person hanged. But they first needed to find the responsible party.

The grandfather clock from the corridor downstairs chimed the hour, and she stopped. Had she been waiting out here for nearly an hour already? And where was Marybeth with the bandages, and Tabitha with the water? These servants were becoming lazy now that Lloyd had died, but she would make sure they still did their duties.

She couldn't stand the waiting, but entering the room would be highly improper. Especially after what Dora had said. And once the servants heard the gossip about what happened this morning at Hanover Hall, she knew they would judge her, even though it wasn't their place to do so.

Since her husband's death, Cassandra had done all she could to repair the reputation that had fallen on the Kentwood name, especially *her* name—but to no avail. Of course, the village believed that she had killed her own husband only two days after they were wed. Almost everyone knew neither bride nor groom were happy about the marriage. But her husband's death had only made people gossip more. Rumors had spread that Cassandra was the one who drove him to drink, and that she encouraged him to go out on the boat with his friends, knowing that other unwed women had been invited to join them. Cassandra found this particular story odd, especially knowing that the servants actually believed it. How she could have allowed her husband to be with his friends that night when she hadn't seen him since their wedding?

When she learned of the marquess's death, she had cried, although they were tears of relief. A few days later, when her husband's solicitor informed her that Collin Worthington would be inheriting the title, she cried again, but out of frustration and anger.

She glared at the closed door. Why had Collin followed her from his brother's wedding today? She prayed he wouldn't die, because she needed to know why he had done all those things to her. Perhaps hearing his story would finally make her put him out of her mind.

Her heart twisted in confusion from everything that had happened, and the emotion angered her. She moved down the stairs to find her *lost* maids. It disturbed her greatly to think that Collin would want to see her. Recalling the way he had gazed at her earlier today also upset her. He actually appeared happy to see her. *Impossible!*

Perhaps he had followed her back to the manor because he wanted to smile at her in that charming way of his that in the past had weakened her body. Did he think he could swoop back into her life now that she was a widow? Well, he had another thing coming if that was his plan.

She would not allow him to hold her against his strong chest, and she would definitely not let him kiss her passionately—or kiss her at all. Collin Worthington was sadly mistaken if that was his purpose in coming to the manor today. She would not give him a moment of her time. He didn't deserve it.

As she neared the kitchen, she heard the maids' high-pitched twittering. Apparently, it was more important to gossip than do their job. When Cassandra reached the door, she heard one of them say her name. Although she shouldn't care what they were saying, she stopped and listened closer.

"I don't know what Lady Kentwood expected from her outburst at Lord Adrian's wedding, but I'm tired of hearing her speak as if she was the one ruined."

Cassandra gritted her teeth. That was Tabitha's voice. This would be that maid's last day working for her, and she would *not* give her a good recommendation.

"After all," Tabitha continued, "any woman should have known about Lord Kentwood's sullied reputation, and because Cassandra didn't turn away the man's attentions, that confirmed to me what I already knew. The woman was nothing but a—"

Cassandra quickly stepped into the room and glared at Tabitha. The maid's mouth hung open and her face paled.

"Lady Kentwood," Marybeth gasped as she curtsied.

Folding her arms, Cassandra narrowed her eyes on the maids. "When the bandages and warm water I requested nearly an hour ago had not been delivered, I decided to see if something terrible had happened to the two of you." She arched an eyebrow. "And now that I know you are still alive, I expect you to bring me what

I need, posthaste." She paused and lifted a chin. "And once you have done that, I expect the two of you to pack your things and leave this place. I don't need your kind of help any further."

She kept her shoulders back and walked out of the kitchen, holding in her dignity. Although some of the servants wanted to take the self-worth from her, she was determined to keep it.

Once she reached the stairs, she hurried up them, faster than when she had descended to find the maids. On the second level, she noticed the guest room door open and Dora exiting. The strain of the afternoon was on the older woman's face, and Cassandra wasn't certain if she was just exhausted, or if something dreadful had happened to Collin.

She hurried to the housekeeper. "Is he still…alive?"

Dora nodded. "The more we moved him while trying to change his clothes, the more his head bled. I had to change the bedding twice."

"How is he now?" Cassandra asked in a tight voice.

Dora shrugged. "At least his head wound isn't bleeding profusely."

The clamoring of feet up the stairs had Cassandra turning to see who was in such a hurry. When Marybeth and Tabitha saw her, they slowed their pace. Thankfully, they carried the items Cassandra needed.

She pointed toward the room. "Take them inside." She turned her focus on the housekeeper. "I will need you to assist me in washing Coll—um, I mean Lord Kentwood's hair and bandaging his head."

The gasps of her servants were louder than Cassandra expected, until she realized they had never met the man who had taken over Lloyd's title. "Forgive me," she explained, "but the injured man is Collin Worthington, the lord who has stepped into my late husband's title."

The maids exchanged wide-eyed gazes before walking into the room. And the driver and footman appeared very uncomfortable, as their stances shifted several times.

"So," she continued as she walked into the room, "when the marquess wakes up, please address him with his new title."

She ignored the mumbles of "yes, my lady" as she took the bucket of warm water from Tabitha and moved it to the side of the bed. Collin's face was still very pale, matching the white men's nightshirt that the housekeeper and the driver had dressed him in.

Dora helped gently move Collin until his head was over the bed. Marybeth laid towels around the area, helping to not get the sheets wet. As the housekeeper held him still, Cassandra washed his hair. The egg-sized swollen cut was on his forehead along his hairline. She prayed he would recover quickly without any lasting damage.

The sooner he was out of here, the better.

After ten minutes, they had Collin's hair washed and mostly dried, and propped his head back on the pillows. His breathing seemed better now. At least he didn't look like death warmed over.

She stood aside as the maids helped Dora clean up the dirty clothes. Once they moved away, Cassandra stepped back to the bed and proceeded to bandage his head.

She glanced toward the door. Tabitha and Marybeth stood against the wall, wringing their hands. Gritting her teeth, Cassandra knew why they were still here. They were going to try to convince her that they were needed in the manor. But she would disagree. She would not put up with their insubordination any longer.

"The two of you are free to leave now," she said, turning her attention back to Collin's bandages.

"Um, Lady Kentwood?" Tabitha said in a shaky voice. "Marybeth and I would like to apologize—"

"I appreciate it," Cassandra interrupted, "but I still want you to leave the manor."

"Um, my lady?" Marybeth said with a catch in her voice. "The rain is terrible, and we don't wish to travel with the roads so poor." She cleared her throat. "We would like to stay until the storm passes."

Cassandra held her breath while she calmed her ire. Perhaps she should be lenient with them for now. "Fine, but once the roads are free to travel on, you two will leave."

"Yes, my lady," they chimed softly.

Seconds later, Cassandra heard them leave and close the door. She breathed a relieved sigh. She would rather not have to look at them while they remained in residence, but at least she would spend most of her time taking care of Collin.

"Lady Kentwood," Dora said. "Was that necessary?"

Cassandra nodded. "Indeed it was. I'm fed up with the rumors in this estate alone. My husband is gone, and it is time I was shown some respect."

"Of course, my lady." Dora sighed and folded her arms, looking at the unconscious man. "He had a nasty blow to the head. I hope he wakes up soon, but I'm certain he will be disoriented for a few days."

"Well, rightly so." Cassandra frowned. "Anyone would feel that way after being hit over the head with a thick tree limb."

"I wonder who could have done such a thing." Dora shook her head.

"I haven't had a chance to ask Bentley what the man who was running away looked like. He just said it was a servant." She looked at the housekeeper. "Do you believe it is one of our servants?"

Dora shrugged. "I wish I could tell you. If it was, maybe they didn't recognize Lord Hanover...um, I mean Lord Kentwood."

"No, I'm sure they didn't know who he was, but it was clear by his clothes that he was a lord. So, why would a servant attack a man of nobility?"

"I hope you find answers soon."

"As do I, Dora."

A groan came from Collin, and Cassandra hitched a breath in surprise. She didn't dare touch him, only because she didn't want him to think she'd had a change of heart. She had meant everything she told him earlier. Even though she would allow him to stay at the manor while he healed, that didn't mean she was going to let him charm her.

His eyelids fluttered open. Immediately, he squinted against the light inside the room, even though it wasn't very bright. Maybe he had a tremendous headache, too. And if that were the case, light would affect it.

"Turn down the lamp, Dora." Cassandra nudged the housekeeper's arm.

The older woman hurried to the lamp on the side table and turned it down.

Cassandra kept her focus on Collin as he stopped squinting and moved his gaze around the room. When his attention fell on her, it stopped. Even through the dim lighting, she could tell he studied her in interest, looking at her from the top of her head, slowly over her face, and to the hands she clasped at her waist. She waited for his cocky grin, only so she could shoot down his hopes.

After a few seconds, he met her eyes. Still, she waited for the smile that had always made her weak in the knees—but that wouldn't happen this time. But it never happened. In fact, his eyes narrowed, and his mouth tugged into a grimace.

"Who are you?" he asked in a hoarse voice.

She held back the snort she wanted to give, only because he genuinely appeared serious. "What do you mean? You know me."

"No, I fear I have never met you before."

The nerve of that man playing innocent. She doubted he acted this way because of Dora being in the room, since he rarely cared what servants thought.

"Perhaps your head injury has made your vision unclear," she replied.

"No, I can see you just fine." He glanced at Dora. "Because I can see that woman as well."

Dora curtsied. "Good afternoon, Lord Kentwood."

His forehead scrunched and his frown deepened. "What did you call me?"

"Lord Kentwood," Dora repeated.

"I'm afraid I don't know that man."

Cassandra rolled her eyes. This needed to stop now. "Collin, have you forgotten you are not Lord Hanover any longer?"

Slowly, he shook his head. The rhythm of his breathing increased, making his chest rise and fall quicker. Panic was his expression now as his breaths escaped his widened nostrils.

"Madam, I…do not know those names."

He blinked as if trying not to cry. This wasn't like Collin. He had played pranks before, and she could tell he wasn't teasing.

"Are you saying you don't remember who you are?"

Liquid filled his eyes no matter how quickly he blinked. "That is exactly what I'm saying. I don't know you, and I certainly don't remember me…or anything."

Cassandra didn't know whether to laugh or cry…or scream with frustration. She tried to feel sorrow, since it was obvious his memory loss was due to his head injury. Sadly, the only thought that flashed through her mind was that his memory lapse would stall her getting retribution.

Or perhaps…this was the very thing she needed to finally put the past to rest.

Chapter Four

CASSANDRA CONTROLLED HER annoyance as she stared at the man on the bed. The nightshirt he wore didn't fit him well, leaving the front unbuttoned enough to see his muscular neck and some of his chest, reminding her how powerfully strong he was. His arms were outside the covers, but the quilt covered the rest of his body. The fire blazed in the hearth, keeping the room's temperature very warm.

The storm clouds had grown darker, which created shadows everywhere. Now she wished she hadn't had Dora turn down the lamp. But then, perhaps it was good that the man with the head injury didn't see how upset she was at the moment.

The housekeeper gasped and quickly covered her mouth. Dora's wide-eyed gaze jumped to Cassandra as she slowly shook her head.

Looking back at Collin, Cassandra breathed slowly. What in heaven's name could she say to a man who had lost his memory? She couldn't scream and throw blame at him anymore, because he wouldn't understand. If the doctor had come, he would instruct her to keep the patient calm.

Then who would keep *her* calm?

"I..." She cleared her dry throat. "I'm sorry you cannot remember, but your name is Collin Worthington, and your title is Lord Kentwood."

His gaze ran over her face again, then down over her gown before bouncing back up to her eyes. Was he trying to remember? Hopefully, this was just a momentary relapse, and he would feel better soon.

She had never been more uncomfortable with him, and she shouldn't act like that now. She was still the lady of the manor, so she must act like it.

"And who are you?" he asked again.

Cassandra wanted to answer, but her mind spun out of control. She couldn't tell him she was the mistress of the manor, especially since this was legally his manor now.

"She is Lady Kentwood," Dora answered.

Cassandra groaned. Perhaps she should have said something first so her housekeeper wouldn't have blurted out the wrong name and confused him.

His eyes widened. "Lady Kentwood? You are…my wife?"

Gritting her teeth, Cassandra fisted her hands by her sides. This was exactly what she didn't want him to think.

She breathed slowly and tried to calm her racing heartbeat. She had loved his baritone voice when they first met, and, even now, hearing it refer to her as his wife sent pleasurable tremors all over her. She really needed to find a way to stop that reaction to him. He hadn't wanted her before, and he would certainly not want her once he regained his memory.

"I'm not your wife. I married your cousin, and his death is why you now have the title."

His stare narrowed. "I must admit, you do look somewhat familiar."

"That is reassuring." She sighed, hoping his memory was returning. "If you think I look familiar then I'm sure it won't be long before you can remember everything."

He smiled, but it wasn't full. "I pray you are correct."

Cassandra fidgeted from one foot to the next as she continually clenched her hands and released them. "Um, is there anything I can have the servants bring you? Are you hungry?"

"I'm grateful for their kindness, but I do not need any food."

"Splendid." Cassandra couldn't stand in one place for much longer. Seeing his face so pale, his hair disheveled, made him appear so helpless. She wasn't used to him this way. He acted like an entirely different man. Thankfully, she knew he wasn't.

"Are you sleepy?" she asked. "My housekeeper and I should leave and let you rest."

He nodded. "I am a little, but you do not have to leave."

"Rest will do you good, I'm sure."

He reached up and touched the bandage around his head. His deep frown returned. "Before you go, will you tell me what happened to me?"

"I wish I knew." Cassandra shrugged. "You were at my estate near the trees, and someone attacked you. None of my servants saw it happen."

"Do you know who attacked me?"

She shook her head. "I haven't had time to question the servants, but I assure you, I shall make it my first act of business once I leave the room. In fact"—she looked at Dora—"will you please gather the servants and have them downstairs in the corridor in one hour so that I can question them?"

"Yes, milady." The housekeeper curtsied and moved out of the room.

The moment the door closed, Cassandra sucked in a ragged breath. She was now alone with the very man who had ruined her life—the man she had told only this morning at his brother's wedding party that she would *never* again be alone with him.

She took another calming breath, telling herself that this time was different. He was injured and in bed, and he couldn't do anything to her anyway. Besides that, he didn't even know his own name. She should be safe...for now.

"Lady Kentwood?" Collin asked in dry voice. "Would you tell me something about my life? It is awful not knowing anything, and literally having a black head, making it impossible to think."

She took a step back. "Well, I'm not sure—"

"Please." He reached out and grasped her wrist, stopping her. "If you would tell me something about my life, perhaps I will start to remember."

Warmth from his touch moved throughout her body, and a pang of guilt wrenched her heart. How could she play the vengeful vixen when he was in this condition? Now she must be kind to him, so when he regained his memory, he would remember her kindness while he was this way. She just didn't have the heart to be vindictive right now.

"Fine, I will."

She slipped out of his grasp. Not wanting to sit on the bed, she moved to the wall and grasped the only wooden chair in the room and carried it next to the bed. She sat, keeping her back straight and hands in her lap.

"You are the eldest of two Worthington brothers. Your younger brother is Adrian. You were the Earl of Hanover, but just recently, you inherited the title Marquess of Kentwood when your cousin, Lloyd—my husband—died in a boating accident."

In silence, she studied his expression. His eyes remained expressionless, which told her he wasn't remembering anything yet. She needed to tell him more. But really, she didn't know that much about him, except for what he had told her when they first met in Bath.

"Your brother, Adrian, was just married. Most people know him by Lord William, but you call him Adrian, which I assume is his middle name."

Slowly, Collin nodded. "That would make sense."

"I have never met him until this morning, though, so I don't know much about him."

"Am I close to him?" Collin asked.

Cassandra wished she knew that answer. But he hadn't confided much of his life when they were growing close during his trip to Bath. "I don't believe you are." She shrugged. "At least, you weren't when I first met you. However, you could be now. Not too long ago, your father purchased a grand manor where you and your brother live."

Keeping his gaze on her, he scrubbed a hand over his chin. "Is my family wealthy?"

She nodded. "Very much so, and now that you have inherited the marquess's lands, you are even wealthier than before."

Collin moved his attention around the room. "And do I own this house?"

Cassandra clenched her jaw. She didn't want this estate to be his. She wanted the estate all to herself now that her husband was dead.

"Yes," she answered in a tight voice. "But this is one of the smaller manors that you own, and it is very secluded, since it is located in the country."

"So, you are pretty much secluded out here?"

"Very much so, my lord."

He exhaled slowly, and a grin touched his mouth. "I think I would quite enjoy the peaceful life of country living." He shrugged. "Of course, I don't know why I feel that way."

Cassandra held her breath, not wanting to release her frustrations. Instead, she must try to convince him that country life was *not* what he wanted.

"Forgive me, my lord," she said, "but from what I know about your lifestyle, I would have to disagree. Living in the country would drive you mad. You would be completely bored."

Confusion crossed his features. "But you live here, correct?"

"Correct."

"And you don't find it boring?"

If he only knew how hilarious that question was. She shifted in her chair. "No, indeed. I prefer the quiet life compared to the hustle and bustle of the busier towns, but only because of how I grew up. My father was a penniless baron, and so I was raised much differently than you were. However, you, my lord, were raised in a wealthy family with a socialite mother who was quite well liked in the *ton's* circles. Your family was always in the spotlight one way or another. You have a respectable family, and you are all expected to make appearances at social events."

His gaze stayed on her, and for several moments, she wondered if he was going to speak again. She hoped he was reconsidering living on the estate, but even if he wasn't, she would do anything in her power to convince him otherwise.

He sighed heavily. "Well, for now as I recover, I think I would like to stay here. I don't remember anything or anyone, and you have such a friendly face. So, if you don't mind, I would like to stay where I feel the most comfortable."

She bunched her hands into fists on her lap, hoping he wouldn't notice that his answer made her upset. But what could she do? She didn't own the estate, and he could go and do as he liked.

Cassandra swallowed hard before clearing her throat. "Oh, of course, my lord. Because the doctor is not here yet, you should stay in bed until you are fully recovered."

"Yes, so right." He lifted his hand and touched the gauze wrapped around his head. "The way I feel right now, I'm surprised my skull isn't split in two."

"I pray you will feel better tomorrow."

"As do I."

Silence passed between them again, making her uncomfortable. If he wouldn't stare at her with those remarkable hazel eyes, perhaps she could tolerate his presence. Perhaps she should go to the kitchen to see if Dora had gathered the rest of the staff. After all, she couldn't put off talking to them another minute.

Cassandra made a move to stand, but he held up his hand, stopping her. "Before you go, will you tell me one more thing?"

"Uh, I suppose there is no harm in that, although you do need your rest."

"Lady Kentwood, would you please tell me about *you*?"

She hitched a breath. Why in heaven's name did he want to know about her? She couldn't possibly tell him much without her anger erupting. But she supposed she could tell him a little. "I, um... What exactly do you want to know?"

Collin stared at her for a few unsettling seconds. It wasn't the silence that bothered her—it was the way his gaze moved slowly over her face, up to her hair, then down again, traveling across her face but then moving lower as he looked over her gown.

She held her breath as her memory opened to a time she wished she could forget. Collin had looked at her in this manner before, and her body had responded as tremors of desire cascaded over her, making her weak in the worst way. Even now as he studied her, she couldn't stop the pounding of her heartbeat and the tingling in her belly. Curse his hide for creating such havoc in her mind until she felt defenseless. Since she had already gone through this with him, she did not want it happening again.

The bedroom door opened, and Dora bustled inside, carrying a tray of food.

"I know you said you weren't hungry," the housekeeper said, "but I thought I should bring this up anyhow, in case you change your mind and I'm not around to bring this to you."

"Thank you, Mrs...." He arched an eyebrow.

"Mrs. Thompson, my lord. I'm the housekeeper."

He smiled. "It is a pleasure to make your acquaintance."

Collin struggled to sit up straighter but was having a difficult time shifting on the bed. Guilt washed over Cassandra for doing nothing, so she stepped closer and placed the pillows behind him. She took hold of his upper arm to assist him.

His gaze flew to hers and locked. Once again, her breath stopped in her throat. She was too close to him, and she needed to move away now before the ice wall around her heart started melting. Under no circumstances could she let that happen.

Trying not to make a scene, she casually released his arm and stepped back. Dora hovered nearby, still holding the plate.

"My lord, do you want me to set it on the table?"

He shook his head. "Perhaps I shall try to eat a little before resting."

"I think that is an excellent idea." Dora placed the tray of food on his lap before moving back toward the door. "Lady Kentwood? I have not been able to gather the staff yet, but Bentley and Riddle are assisting me."

"Splendid." Cassandra sighed with relief, knowing she would finally have a good excuse to leave the room.

"Is there anything else you need, milady?" Dora asked.

"No. That is all, Mrs. Thompson." As soon as Cassandra said the words, she wished she could recant them. She really didn't want to be in the bedroom alone with Collin. And now she couldn't tell him she was meeting with the household staff right away, because he knew differently.

The servant walked out of the room and closed the door. Cassandra swallowed hard, trying to moisten her suddenly dry throat. Her mind spun with excuses to give him to leave. Being alone with him was unhealthy.

Hesitantly, she looked at Collin. He had taken a spoonful of stew, but his attention was on her. His throat jumped in a swallow, and he smiled.

"You must compliment your cook. This stew is delicious."

"Yes, I'll let her know." Cassandra fidgeted, wringing her hands against her middle.

"Lady Kentwood, could you please tell me how we met? I'm sure my memory would return if you could feed it with something that happened in my life."

Inwardly, she groaned. Could she really tell him how they met without appearing like a giddy schoolgirl? Telling him about that dreadful day when they were supposed to meet at the abandoned cottage would be difficult. She definitely wouldn't be able to hold her anger then. But hopefully, he would have recovered his memories at that point. She could only pray that was what would happen.

Nodding, she returned to her chair. He continued to eat, but his gaze only left her face for a second to look at his bowl of stew before coming back to her.

Oh, Lord, please help me!

Chapter Five

Thirteen months earlier

"TWO MEN ARE coming this way!"

The squeal from the sixteen-year-old Olivia and the quick footsteps on the wooden floor had Cassandra pausing in the middle of playing one of Mozart's pieces on the pianoforte. She spun on the stool and glanced at her sister standing by the window, wringing her hands. Cassandra looked past her sibling to see what the commotion was about. Even from a distance, it was obvious the two men were nicely dressed, and walked straight and tall. She would bet they were noblemen.

Shaking her head, she pushed the silly notion from her head. *Noblemen?* Although her grandfather had been a baron, his firstborn son and family had been shunned from Society because of the Featherstones' gambling habits. Cassandra's family was impoverished, and it was quite embarrassing to have anyone wealthy drop by to visit them. It surprised her, since it had never happened. Until now.

Olivia gawked at the men who slowly walked toward their home. She sucked in a breath and ran her hands over her ringlets of blonde hair before frantically pulling on the ties of the apron around her waist.

"Cassandra, I believe they are lords."

Olivia struggled with the apron, so Cassandra moved away from the musical instrument and stepped behind her younger sister to finish removing the garment.

"Liv, you need to calm down and stop making a spectacle of yourself." She pulled her sister's elbow, moving her away from their visitors' view. "And for heaven's sake, you don't need to let them know you have been watching out the window this whole time."

"What do you think they are doing? Why would they come to see us?" Olivia's brown eyes twinkled with excitement.

"I honestly believe they are lost." Cassandra gave a sharp nod. "Why else would two gentlemen be coming toward our home without a proper invitation?"

"I wonder why they aren't in a carriage," Olivia muttered, and peered out the window again.

Cassandra pulled on her sister's arm, getting her attention. "They are nearly here. Father needs to be informed. Make haste, before the men reach our porch."

Olivia rushed out of the parlor and clambered up the stairs, calling for their pa in a high-pitched voice. Cassandra grimaced. Only the deaf and deceased would not be able to hear such a ruckus. Then again, as loud as her sister was, maybe that class of people could hear anyway.

Releasing a nervous breath, Cassandra smoothed her palms over the outdated material of her blue day dress. Funds had been extremely hard to come by, and her mother tried her best to adjust the girls' dresses each year. Unfortunately, Cassandra had almost outgrown her clothes. Her bosom was nearly too large for the bodice.

A loud knock rattled the front door, making Cassandra jump. Her heartbeat quickened. She, too, would like to know what these two men were doing out in the middle of nowhere and without a carriage.

Slowly, she stepped toward the door, keeping her shoulders straight and trying to at least appear as though she had been raised by a proper father, despite her shabby attire. She stopped, inhaled a refreshing breath to calm her fiercely beating heart, and opened the door.

When she got her first look at the two gentlemen, she nearly sighed aloud. Both were tall, but the man with wavy sandy-blond hair had wider shoulders. Both were handsome, but the more slender man with brown hair wasn't scowling like his friend, which, in her opinion, made him the better looking of the two.

"Pardon our unannounced visit," the man with brown hair said, bowing slightly. "I'm Lord Kentwood, and this is Lord Hanover."

She curtsied. It surprised her that the man with broader shoulders hadn't shown her respect by bowing. "It is a pleasure to meet you. My father is Baron Featherstone. I'm his daughter, Miss Featherstone."

Lord Kentwood smiled. "The pleasure is all ours, I assure you."

She tried not to let his compliment get to her. After all, she was certain this smooth-talking lord was a rogue, as was his friend. But it didn't matter—their very presence caused her mind to go blank. Not often did she get the opportunity to converse with handsome, titled men.

"Miss Featherstone," Lord Kentwood continued, "Lord Hanover and I are stranded. Our carriage wheel is broken, and we are in hopes that your father will be able to help us out of our predicament."

A gust of wind came out of nowhere, pushing the men from behind. Lord Hanover stumbled forward, practically falling against her. His large hands grasped her shoulders, and his head bumped against hers. A sharp pain rushed through her temples, and she groaned.

"Pardon me, Miss Featherstone," the lord muttered, and quickly withdrew, moving back on the porch. "Forgive me for knocking into you. It was very ill-mannered of me."

Feeling uncomfortable from the brief contact, she forced a

laugh. "It was not your fault, my lord. We must put the blame on the wind."

He nodded, but the scowl remained on his face. Cassandra could tell this man was not happy about their situation. Either that, or touching a penniless waif disgusted him more than he had realized. However, Lord Kentwood's eyes gleamed with mirth, and he chuckled over his friend's clumsiness. Indeed, this lord was much flirtier. She enjoyed his cheerful attitude.

"Please," Cassandra said, moving back and opening the door wider, "why don't you come inside, out of the wind?" She glanced at the sky. Gray clouds billowed in the distance. "It appears a storm is brewing."

Just as the two men entered, the stairs creaked as her pa and two brothers scampered down the stairs, heading toward them. Her older brother, Charles, tripped and almost fell into their father. Thankfully, Charles righted himself before causing them to all roll down the steps.

Cassandra silently groaned. They *had* been raised properly, but an outsider wouldn't be able to notice, especially if they were wealthy. Sometimes, she wondered why her family didn't try to live better.

"My lords," Cassandra said, "let me introduce you to my father, Baron Featherstone."

The lords bowed to her father, and he returned the gesture. It surprised her that Lord Hanover bowed at all. Apparently, it was only lowly women he didn't show his respect to.

As her father introduced his two sons, Charles and Jacob, Cassandra noticed Olivia gracefully making her way down the stairs as her gaze stayed on their visitors. She sashayed toward Cassandra and stopped right beside her.

Biting her inner cheek, Cassandra tried not to laugh. Her sister had taken the time to brush out her ringlets to give their visitors the impression she was a woman instead of a girl. It must have worked, because Olivia gained attention from both lords.

"I heard you tell my daughter that your carriage broke down

not too far from here." The baron folded his arms across his chest. "If you would like my boys to take a look at it—"

"How thoughtful of you," Lord Kentwood said. "However, all we ask is the use of your servants for now."

Cassandra held her breath. A small gasp escaped Olivia's throat and her face paled. Cassandra cursed her family's fate. Servants? The Featherstone family hadn't been fortunate enough to have servants for the past five years.

"I, um…" Her father cleared his throat, shifting from one foot to the other. "Unfortunately, my servants… Um, well… You see, they are not here at the moment."

Olivia's gaze swung to Cassandra, and the girl's eyes were wide with terror. Cassandra clenched her teeth. *Father is lying to them!* Obviously, her parent had forgotten that he had been raised a titled lord as well.

"None of them are here?" Lord Kentwood asked in a tone laced with skepticism.

Her father laughed, shaking his head. "I only have a few, you see, and there was a death in their family, so I released them from their duties for a few days."

Lord Hanover continued to stare at Cassandra's father in doubt, but Lord Kentwood's gaze shone with appreciation. The two men were completely opposite, but she feared they both knew how to deceive people, just as most men of the realm.

"Baron Featherstone, you certainly have a giving heart," Lord Kentwood remarked.

The baron's chest seemed to swell as a grin stretched over his face. He turned to Charles and Jacob. "Collect the tools from the shed and we shall go with these fine gentlemen to fix their carriage."

"Yes, Pa," both Charles and Jacob answered simultaneously before rushing past, heading out the back way.

Pa looked at Cassandra. "You and Olivia start making dinner. I'm sure these men will be hungry by the time we are finished."

"Yes, Pa." Cassandra glanced at the two lords again. Only

Lord Kentwood smiled. The other lord appeared bored and perhaps a bit impatient. That man would be difficult to tolerate, and she hoped they didn't plan on staying long.

As Cassandra turned toward the kitchen, Olivia spun around and followed. When they were both inside the room, Olivia released a heavy breath and placed her hand to her chest.

"I don't think I have ever seen more handsome men in my life." She collapsed dramatically on the counter and smiled dreamily. "And to think they are going to have supper with us."

Cassandra rolled her eyes. "Not if you don't get your head out of the clouds and help me."

Olivia straightened slowly. "Ma will be home soon, and she can do it."

"Liv, I suggest you shake those impure thoughts out of your head now."

Olivia's eyes widened as a blush covered her face. "I don't know what you're talking about."

"Those men out there are true lords, which means they are not going to give us a second look." Cassandra swished her hand through the air. "They have eyes, and I'm sure they can see just how poor we are. In fact"—she stepped closer to her sister—"once they discover Pa lied to them about our so-called servants, those two handsome lords will not want anything more to do with our lying father or his family."

Frowning, Olivia leaned her hip against the counter. "Do you think we are going to turn into spinsters?"

A feeling of desperate longing squeezed Cassandra's heart. She had worried that her father's mistakes would keep her and Olivia from finding good husbands. Spinsterhood was in her future. The only way they would ever become married was by finding a farmer and convincing him that they could help with the farm, since that was what Cassandra and her sister had been doing since the servants left.

Ma had tried to bring up her daughters to respect others and have giving hearts. She had taught them how to stay cheerful even through the times that appeared bad, such as now. Grandfather Featherstone hadn't been wealthy, but he made do with what he had, which was passed to Cassandra's father. Unfortunately, her reckless father wanted more from life, which was why he started gambling. At least now he didn't have any money left to gamble.

A slight ache throbbed in Cassandra's head. "I pray that won't happen to us, Liv. We deserve to find good husbands. I don't want to live here the rest of my life, but it is up to us to find our own way. After all, I still believe in miracles."

Or, at least, she *wanted* to believe.

Chapter Six

THAT EVENING, CASSANDRA picked at the food on her plate, not really in the mood to eat. Her family and their two invited guests sat around the table for supper. Pa and her two brothers appeared exhausted after fixing the lords' carriage, and of course, the two lords hadn't broken a sweat—unless it was because they had walked too fast on their way to repair the vehicle.

Lord Kentwood took up most of the conversation, just as he had done when they first met. He had many stories to tell, which enthralled her family, especially Cassandra's siblings. She enjoyed hearing the stories as well, but Lord Hanover had captured her attention more. The man's gaze wandered around their meager furnishings in disgust, and she couldn't help but feel offended. She loathed men who were so arrogant that they couldn't understand those who were in a lower class. She wanted to say something or slap his expression right off his face. But she had been raised right, which meant she would say nothing.

At least Lord Kentwood was being polite, even though by now, the men would have figured out the Featherstones' lowly circumstances. The handsome lord with brown hair had certainly better manners than his friend, and her respect for the man grew.

Ma hadn't seemed to notice the way the uppity Lord Hanover was acting. She fawned over both men as if she had never served food to guests in her house before. At least Cassandra heard the snooty lord thank her mother for her kind hospitality, and for the tasty food. Cassandra tried not to let it disturb her that her mother never once acknowledged that the meal was mainly prepared by the baron's daughters and *not* the baroness.

Cassandra nibbled on her roll and watched Lord Hanover take another sip of wine. Slowly, his gaze lifted and moved straight to her. Surprised that he would even look at her, she sucked in a breath, and nearly choked. Trying not to show her inability to breathe for a few seconds, she grabbed her glass and forced the wine down her throat—as daintily as possible, of course.

Once she felt she had it under control, she peeked toward Lord Hanover again. His attention was still on her. This time, his gaze had narrowed, but thankfully, he didn't appear to be disgusted now. At the moment, she wasn't certain exactly what kind of expression he wore. Was he feeling pleasant or annoyed?

The room grew quiet as everyone continued with their meal. She pretended to eat, but nobody really noticed, which was how she wanted it, because she had never enjoyed being the center of attention. Yet whenever she peeked toward Lord Hanover, his focus was still on her.

She shifted in her seat, feeling extremely uncomfortable. If only they could return to how they treated each other earlier, with indifference and no respect for the other. Perhaps he was getting revenge on her because she had been keeping an eye on him just to see how disgusted he acted.

She swallowed the small amount of food in her mouth, slower this time so as not to choke. Tightening her fingers around the fork, she silently counted to ten, trying to calm herself. Her palm moistened, and her throat turned dry. Why was he still staring? And how could she stop him? Unless perhaps it was time to strike up a conversation with him. At least that might get the others around the table talking and, in the process, teach him that looking at her in such a way would only make her irritable.

Straightening her shoulders, she sat up and aimed her gaze at him, but as she opened her mouth to speak, he cleared his throat.

"Miss Featherstone, I believe you and your sister helped prepare the meal, correct?"

His voice was smooth as silk, and surprisingly, not judgmental. Not yet, anyway. Either that or he knew how to hold it inside for the moment.

She nodded. "Indeed we did, my lord."

"I must say"—he glanced briefly at his potatoes—"I have never eaten anything so tasty. I have been to Paris and even Ireland, but never has a mere potato tasted so heavenly."

His compliment caught her off guard. Up until now, she didn't believe he knew how to be kind. Her thoughts stumbled, and she wasn't certain if he was being rude or complimentary.

"Uh, I thank you, my lord."

He lifted his glass of wine to her. "I commend you for having such a rare talent."

Even as perplexed as she felt right now, she still managed a smile. "Knowing that you have enjoyed the dish makes me very happy."

Pa wiped the linen napkin across his mouth before leaning forward slightly, zeroing his gaze on Lord Hanover. "My daughter is extremely talented. You should hear her on the pianoforte. And she sings."

Embarrassment swept over Cassandra, making her face hot. She really wished her father hadn't said that. She hated the attention everyone was giving her. Although she was grateful her father didn't shame her, she still thought he exaggerated her accomplishments.

Lord Hanover's eyebrows lifted as his expression changed to one of curiosity. "You play?"

"Yes." She licked her suddenly dry lips. "However, I doubt I'm as good as my father makes it sound."

"Do you have a pianoforte?" Lord Hanover asked.

"Indeed we do," Cassandra's mother quickly answered. "It's

in the music room. Would you like to hear her play, my lord?"

He kept his gaze on her as he slowly nodded. "I think I would enjoy that very much."

Cassandra swallowed the lump of terror rising in her dry throat. "Do you also play, my lord?"

His smile widened. She couldn't believe how handsome that made him. Now she wished he would return to being irritable. At least she could control her thoughts when he annoyed her.

"I do, Miss Featherstone. I happen to enjoy music."

She nodded. "As do I. There are times when music is the only way to soothe my nerves."

"I agree." His smile widened. "I have found nothing better."

Seeing the gleam in his eyes, and hearing the smoothness of his deep voice, caused her heartbeat to quicken, making her feel breathless. Nothing like this had ever happened in her twenty-two years. Her face grew even warmer, too. Hopefully, nobody noticed how Lord Hanover had affected her, because she needed to figure out a way to keep it from happening again. Feeling this way was *not* acceptable.

"Miss Featherstone," Lord Kentwood spoke up. "I would also like to hear you play." He wiped the linen napkin across his mouth before setting it on his empty plate and pushing away from the table. "Would you mind performing for us now?"

On cue, everyone followed the lord's lead and stood. Cassandra didn't have any qualms about playing at a moment's notice, but she felt bad for not eating more than she had. In her family's impoverished circumstances, she hated to waste food.

Sighing in defeat, she stood and walked behind the group toward the music room. Lord Hanover seemed not to be in a hurry, and because he walked so slowly, everyone passed him until she had caught up to him. He really was a tall man, and although she detested some of his haughtiness, she couldn't discount his handsome appearance, or his lovely hazel eyes. Not only that, but he had a nice smile—when he wasn't forcing it, of course.

"Lord Hanover," she said, which captured his attention. "I would very much like to hear you play, as well."

Nodding, he grinned. "I'm sure I'm not anywhere as good as you, but I shall play if that will make you happy."

Her heartbeat skipped. *He wants to make me happy?* Confusion filled her as she tore her gaze away from him and moved toward the pianoforte. Why was he all of a sudden being nice to her? The way he had been acting since they first arrived made her aware of what he must think of their lowly situation. So, why had he changed his mind?

Yet her mind warned her to be wary. Her family had been hurt before by so-called *noble*men, and she was certain it would happen again. She must not trust either of their visitors.

Cassandra sat at the pianoforte. The selection she decided upon was one she had memorized years ago. She rested her fingers on the keys as her memory opened. While she played, she could see the expressions from across the musical instrument of those who were nearby. Lord Hanover stood directly in her view, and it was hard not to stare at him while playing the ballad she had fallen in love with years ago after first hearing her mother play the piece. The dreaminess in Lord Hanover's eyes, and the softness of his smile, let her know he was pleased with what he heard.

Her heart softened, even though she shouldn't allow it to. Yet seeing him this way made her wish for a better life—a life where a man would fall in love with her because of the woman she was and overlook her pitiful family's situation.

As soon as she was finished, everyone applauded, but she could hear Lord Hanover clap louder than the others. She stood and curtsied before motioning with her hand for him to come play the pianoforte. The others encouraged him, and it didn't take him long to give in and take his seat on the stool. The moment his fingers flew across the keys, her heart flipped with excitement. He played magnificently, and she was spellbound. What she wouldn't give to have more lessons so that she could learn to make her fingers move that fast.

When he finished, she sighed from happiness and disappointment. She didn't want it to end, but she joined in the clapping with everyone else. She was certain she clapped the loudest from his amazing performance.

It didn't take long before they split into groups and chatted for the next little while. She stood next to Lord Hanover, listening to his childhood stories about when his mother had him play the pianoforte in front of her friends and at social gatherings. He admitted to being embarrassed from all the attention, and wishing he could only play for his own love of music. It surprised Cassandra that she shared these emotions with him, but she certainly wouldn't admit it.

Another thing that stunned her was seeing how humorous he was. She found herself laughing too many times, but thankfully, her sister and brothers found him just as entertaining, so she didn't stand out.

But the most startling thing of all was that his deep voice made her heart pitter-patter faster than normal. Slowly, throughout the evening, her infatuation for him grew. Even though Cassandra kept telling herself there was no way a man like Lord Hanover would consider her as a wife, she still wanted to believe that he found her interesting. She wouldn't mind if he found her pretty, as well, but that might be pushing her hopes a little too far.

When he looked at her, his eyes twinkled. They hadn't done that when they first met. So perhaps he was feeling the attraction between them. Then again, it was probably all her imagination. After all, he had met—and probably courted—many beautiful women that were more talented than Cassandra, whereas she had only had a schoolgirl crush on a few boys in her life, nothing like she was feeling now.

Jacob took over the conversation, and for the life of her, Cassandra couldn't keep her mind on what her brother was saying. Instead, she studied Lord Hanover's handsome face. He was definitely one finely built man, one she never thought she would meet. And now that he stood so close, it was nearly impossible not to want to touch his arms just to see if they were as muscular as they appeared. Her palms itched to caress his rugged chin to see if the skin was coarse or smooth. And heaven help her, but she wanted to thread her fingers through his lovely, wavy sandy-blond hair just to see if he liked women doing that to him.

Lord Hanover seemed to be listening to her brother, but suddenly, his gaze shifted and met hers. A teasing smile stretched across his face, as if he knew what she had been thinking. She prayed the look of admiration wasn't etched on her face the way it was on her siblings' expressions.

Heat consumed her cheeks, then slowly spread down her neck and throughout her body. *Where is my fan?* Yet the hotter her face became, the more she realized a mere fan would not cool her enough. An ice-cold pond, or even a bank of snow, might be the only thing that would calm her down.

She touched her brother's arm, stopping him in mid-sentence. "Jacob, excuse me, but I need to step outside. It is very stuffy in this room, and—"

"What a splendid idea," Lord Hanover said. "Why don't we all take a stroll outside and get some fresh air?"

"I, uh…" Jacob stuttered as his attention moved between Lord Hanover and her. "I suppose we could do that, my lord."

Cassandra didn't wait to ask for anyone else's approval before she led the way toward the front door. Holding her breath, she waited for the moment the cooler air would touch her cheeks and remove the heat from her body.

Just before she could reach for the doorknob, Lord Hanover reached in front of her, grasping the knob and opening the door. She gave him a polite smile and hurried outside. After taking five steps away from the house, she closed her eyes and breathed deeply. Just as she suspected, the cooler air helped. Of course, their walk wouldn't be very long, because she suspected she would become chilled soon, since she hadn't thought to first grab her shawl.

"What a beautiful night." Lord Hanover's voice was so close.

She hitched a breath and swung her head to look over her shoulder. The handsome man walked too close but stared up at the night sky.

"I notice the rainstorm didn't last very long," he continued.

"Yes, thankfully." She peeked up, noticing the twinkling stars against the sky's dark canvas. If not for the handsome man beside her, she would have been satisfied with the sky. When she returned her focus to him, she realized her sister and brother were not out with them. "Where are the others?"

Lord Hanover looked back at the manor. "I think I heard your sister mention fetching her shawl, and your brother said something about finding a lantern to light our way."

"Oh dear." Her heartbeat quickened. *They were alone.*

His gaze met hers, and he smiled. "But that will give me time to do something I have been wanting to do since I heard your remarkable performance on the pianoforte."

She sucked in a breath. Her body shook from the unknown, but at the same time, she wondered if he wanted to kiss her. As ridiculous as it seemed, she had thought of how it might feel to kiss someone so blindingly attractive. Yet why would he think the same way? Just because he enjoyed her performance, that didn't mean he wanted to kiss a penniless farmer's daughter.

Chapter Seven

CASSANDRA'S HEART WHACKED crazily against her ribs, threatening to break them—or at least bruise her severely. Why had she put that insane idea into her mind? Now she couldn't think straight. But it didn't matter. She wouldn't allow him to kiss her even if he wanted, and of course he didn't. It was too soon to become personal with a man who was still a stranger to her.

When Lord Hanover turned away from her and moved to the nearest rosebush, she realized a kiss wasn't what he had in mind. Instead, he plucked a lavender rose from the bush and presented it to her. Disappointment washed over her, yet her heart melted from his gesture.

"For you, my lovely Miss Featherstone."

Her hand trembled slightly as she took the rose from him. Did he realize what the meaning was behind each colored rose? Most men of nobility were taught, just as women were. But if he knew, then why would he bring her a lavender rose? The closer bush would have been the red roses, but he stepped past that to get her the purple flower.

He obviously wasn't trying to tell her he *loved* her, which was what this color represented. After all, they barely knew each other. But another meaning for the lavender rose was that he was eager to grow their relationship.

Once again, she found the idea preposterous. She must remember what she had told her sister earlier this evening. Cassandra's head should not be in the clouds. Not with this man.

"I…" Her tight throat made her voice sound too scratchy, so she swallowed hard. "I thank you, my lord."

"I beg you will call me Collin," he said.

The thumping of her heart accelerated. "Then you must call me Cassandra."

"Indeed I shall, since you have a lovely name." He motioned to the flower. "I pray your mother won't get upset that I plucked the rose from her garden."

"Of course not. Olivia and I pick flowers all the time."

His smile widened as he turned and offered her his elbow. "Would you allow me to escort you around the yard, my sweet Cassandra?"

As she hooked her hand around his elbow, she became breathless. Being this close to him wrought havoc inside of her, and she scarcely knew how to control these odd feelings. "Of course I will…Collin." Embarrassment caused heat to climb to her cheeks. She had nearly sighed his name.

The way she acted was quite embarrassing, and one way or another, she needed to get a grip on these chaotic emotions. She must remember how annoyingly disgusted he had been there at the beginning, and how he couldn't even bow when she had curtsied. Also, she should remind herself that he was probably a rogue and only had one thing in mind, which, of course, she would not let him have.

With her mind becoming mushy, she must think of a conversation topic. That could keep her on track…she hoped.

"Collin, what are you and Lord Kentwood doing in Bath?"

He shrugged as they walked around the rose garden. "Bath was just somewhere my cousin and I wanted to visit for a spell."

She glanced at his profile. It didn't matter which way he faced—he was still one fine-looking man. "Your cousin came with you?"

He turned his face and met her gaze. "My cousin is Lord Kentwood."

She chuckled. "I wouldn't have guessed it. You two look nothing alike."

"Kentwood is from my mother's side of the family, and I take after my father's side—the Worthingtons."

"You are a Worthington?"

He arched an eyebrow. "You seem surprised."

"I have heard of the Worthington lords, believe it or not."

"I hope you have heard good things."

She laughed loudly, then quickly stopped herself and placed a hand over her mouth. "Forgive me for that outburst."

He tilted his head and narrowed his eyes. "Now I'm most curious to why you acted that way."

"How close a relation are you to Lord Gavin Worthington?"

His smile widened. "He is one of my close cousins."

"Oh dear." All humor left her. "Then perhaps I shouldn't say anything."

"No, please, go on." He rested his hand over her fingers that still held on to his arm. "I enjoy hearing about my cousins' exploits, whether good or bad."

"Well, I can assure you, this isn't one of Lord Gavin's good stories."

"Tell me anyway."

"Lord Gavin seduced my friend's aunt."

"Her *aunt?*" He paused briefly. "How old was this lady's aunt?"

"She was nearing her thirtieth birthday, but she looked much younger."

Collin nodded. "Then I'm pleased to hear he didn't seduce an old woman."

Cassandra tilted back her head and laughed loudly again, not able to control it. She liked that Collin's comments could catch her off guard. "Oh, that is very humorous, especially when I actually pictured it in my mind."

"I must admit that most of my cousins are rogues." He shrugged one shoulder. "The truth is, most of the Worthington men hold some type of scandalous title."

She knew it, but what she didn't know was if this included Collin. "What about you? What title do you hold?"

"Oh, my sweet Cassandra, I fear that telling you would ruin your opinion of me."

"Indeed? What kind of opinion do you think I have?"

Grinning, he touched a finger to her nose. "This morning, you thought I was arrogant, and this evening while you played for the group, you thought me charming. I would rather you think of me as amiable."

It frustrated her that he wouldn't tell her, but she also knew that he was flirty, which meant he had a roguish personality, just like his cousins.

As he led them away from her mother's flower garden, the voices of Jacob and Olivia leaving the house let Cassandra know her private stroll with Lord Hanover would be over soon. She nearly sighed with relief. She wasn't used to being strong and keeping her emotions in check. But seconds later, she heard more voices, and she peeked over her shoulder just as her parents and Lord Kentwood exited the house.

"Hanover, a moment, please," Lord Kentwood said loudly, raising his hand.

When Cassandra's escort stopped and faced his friend, her hopes sank. The expression on the other man's face wasn't very encouraging. She couldn't tell if Lord Kentwood was upset or just impatient.

"Hanover," Lord Kentwood said as he reached them. "Forgive me for cutting this evening short, but I just remembered another function I had agreed to attend this evening." His gaze shifted to Cassandra. "I hope you forgive me as well."

Slowly, she released her hold of Lord Hanover's arm. Although disappointed that they hadn't had more time together, she realized how fortunate it was that he had paid her some attention.

After tonight, she doubted she would see him again. Both men had mentioned coming to Bath on holiday, which meant they would soon leave. There would be no reason to further their acquaintance with the lowly Featherstone family.

Collin turned and bowed to her. "It was a pleasure to meet you, Miss Featherstone."

"The pleasure was all mine, Lord Hanover."

Once the lords said their goodbyes, they climbed inside their coach and drove away. Although this was a night Cassandra would never forget, she would return to being the reclusive maiden her father had made her into and prepare for spinsterhood.

COLLIN SAT IN the coach, staring out the window, but the only things he could see were Cassandra's wide blue eyes. When she smiled or laughed, they sparkled like the sun hitting an ocean on a clear day.

Exhaling slowly, he relaxed on the seat, remembering her slightly disheveled appearance when he had first looked at her when she opened the door to greet him and Kentwood. Her blonde hair wasn't as smooth as most women he knew, and her worn gown needed ironing.

She had seemed very hesitant and leery of them both. He knew his attitude hadn't been exemplary at that time, due to the carriage breaking down, as well as the infuriating missive that had been delivered from his father this morning. Needless to say, Collin hadn't been in good spirits when arriving at the Featherstone home.

Of course, he should be used to how his father dealt with his two wayward sons. Between Collin and his younger brother, Adrian was the one who had gotten into trouble more. Still, Father had decided to buy a manor to house his sons in hopes that the brothers would get along and become responsible adults.

Again, Collin thought Adrian was the one who needed this lesson more. He wasn't looking forward to returning home and finding his belongings had already been moved into the new manor. Nor was he hopeful that he and his brother would become closer. The distance between them was what kept them both alive.

The coach's wheel hit a rock, making the vehicle tilt slightly, snapping Collin from his thoughts. Although he didn't want to think of his father's disturbing news, he wouldn't mind imagining being with Cassandra again.

He had sorely misjudged her, even though he had her family pegged right from the start. However, Cassandra was vastly different. She actually wanted to portray a well-bred lady, whereas the rest of the family showed Collin that they had somehow lost their upbringing during their impoverished time.

He enjoyed Cassandra's company, and he would cherish the sound of her playing the pianoforte even if they never saw each other again. Although she hadn't said anything about it to him, he could see her love for music. He could relate to this emotion, and he wouldn't mind talking with her about it. A few times while she played, her eyes closed, and the pleasant expression on her pretty face let him know how much she enjoyed the piece.

And at the table, during their brief conversation, he noticed how well-mannered she was, and certainly well conversed. Another thing he noticed was that she watched him even though she tried to pretend she didn't. Knowing that she shot him invisible daggers with her glare after they first met, and then to catch her studying him, had caught his interest.

Most women fell all over themselves and were complete ninnies to meet him and capture his attention, but Cassandra was exactly opposite. At first, it had bothered him, since he had finally met a woman who didn't like him right away, but then as he communicated with her more and she started to smile, he wanted more. It was too bad that Kentwood had remembered a function they needed to attend…

Wait. That wasn't right.

Collin snapped alert, trying to remember his and Kentwood's agenda this evening. He and his cousin Lloyd had planned their holiday to Bath together, but Collin didn't think they had anything to do tonight. In fact, he recalled his cousin telling him they would just find a gaming hall and play cards.

"Kentwood?" he asked, pulling his focus from the window to stare at the man sitting across from him.

Lloyd's eyes snapped open, and he straightened. Apparently, Collin's cousin had fallen asleep.

"Yes?"

"Refresh my memory, but what other engagement do we have tonight?"

Lloyd scratched his chin. "What do you mean?"

Collin rolled his eyes. "You told the Featherstones that we had a previous engagement, did you not?"

"Indeed I did." Lloyd folded his arms and leaned back in the seat again. "I needed to say something to get us away from those ill-mannered people."

"Ill-mannered?" Collin shook his head. "If you thought that way about them, why did you agree to have supper with them? After all, you were the one who answered for both of us."

Lloyd blew out an irritated breath. "Because I knew we needed to be fed before we left. We have a big game tonight, and I didn't want to waste time finding a place to dine for the evening meal."

"I could have been just fine without the game. You know I don't enjoy gambling."

Lloyd snickered. "That is only because you aren't good at it."

"It is because I have never been interested in the sport."

"Well, nevertheless, I needed to say something to get us out of there." Lloyd shrugged. "Besides, I could tell Miss Featherstone was aiming her sights on you. I didn't want you to be her next conquest."

"If you must know, cousin, I was enjoying myself with her."

Lloyd shook his head. "Which is another reason I needed to get you away. Women like that are only good for two things, and marriage isn't one of them."

Collin fisted his hands. He wished his cousin would start thinking of other people's feelings once in a while. "Miss Featherstone isn't like most women. In fact, I might return to visit with her again."

Lloyd narrowed his eyes. "Mark my words, if you do, she will trap you into marriage. I have seen it done too many times, and the farther away we get from women like that, the better we are."

Not often did Collin disagree with Kentwood, but this would be the exception.

Chapter Eight

CASSANDRA STARED AT her reflection in the mirror and scowled. What was Aunt Frances thinking to have her brother's lowly family attend a masked ball at the old woman's country manor? She knew they couldn't afford new clothes, which meant they would show up wearing rags, while everyone else in attendance would be dressed in fine silks and satins.

When Father had received the invitation a week ago, Cassandra tried to argue with her parents that they should not go. She hated to be seen in public anyway, especially at the social events that they were rarely invited to. She didn't like how people looked at them—the same way Collin Worthington had looked at her when she opened the door and let him and his cousin inside the house two days ago.

Her heart sank. Why couldn't she stop thinking about that man? She had been despondent since he and Lord Kentwood left. Although it had been refreshing to receive such wonderful attention from the handsome lord, now that they were gone, she realized—more than ever—that she would never fall in love. She and her sister would become spinsters.

She wished the lords hadn't graced the Featherstone house with their presence. Then she would have continued on with her humdrum life of being satisfied with her future. But now she wanted more.

Sighing heavily, she frowned and gazed over her gown. Mother had tried to fix one of Cassandra's old gowns for the ball, and although it didn't look as horrendous as the one she wore while Lord Hanover and Lord Kentwood were there for dinner, tonight's gown wasn't fancy enough to wear to a masked ball, either.

She blinked away the tears threatening to spring forth. Crying wouldn't make things any better, so why waste the effort? It wasn't as though she craved riches, but if only they had enough money for new clothes once in a while, or at least for good food. They didn't have to live like kings, but she was tired of living like paupers.

Inhaling deeply, she slowly smoothed her palms along the deep blue gown as she tried to breathe away her frustration. Black lace trimmed the heart-shaped bodice and off-the-shoulder sleeves as well as the hem of the gown. She fixed her hair in ringlets instead of coiling it in a bun. Because the bulk fell past her shoulders, she was certain the curl would be gone within an hour.

Her grandmother's gold locket circled her neck, and matching gold earbobs hung from her earlobes. These pieces of jewelry were the only things of value because they came from the grandmother who had been the world to Cassandra, but died seven years ago.

She sighed again as her frown deepened. Aunt Frances would never be embarrassed with her penniless relatives in attendance. Several times, Cassandra had heard the old woman tell her snooty friends that she was *helping* her poor brother and his family. Cassandra's family was nothing but her charity, according to Aunt's Frances's friends, who looked up to the woman for being so generous. Cassandra was just itching to tell them the truth. The old woman had never given them a shilling.

Sadly, it didn't matter to Cassandra's parents. This was their only time to hobnob with nobility.

Her name was called from downstairs. The family was ready to leave and waiting on her. Why couldn't they see that they would be a laughingstock once they arrived at Aunt Frances's manor?

Groaning, she turned and grabbed her cloak before exiting her room. As always, her brothers were bickering about some mundane thing, and her sister stood by the window, dreamily looking out as she twirled a ringlet of hair around her finger.

"Oh, there you are," Mother said. "Let us leave. I hate to be late."

Cassandra would rather be late than early. The more people who were at the party, the more she could make herself invisible.

The ride to the party was miserable, since she had to listen to her sister's excitement. Although this was the first masked ball they had been invited to, it wasn't the first gathering at their aunt's manor. Why was Cassandra the only one to see what their aunt's true purpose was for inviting the family who had fallen away from Society?

Once they reached their destination and the coach stopped, she climbed out with the assistance of Jacob and waited as her parents exited the vehicle. She scanned the manor looming before her, knowing she would never be mistress of such a fine home. But it didn't matter, just as long as she was the mistress of *some* home, married to a good man, and they could raise children.

As they waited with the crowd of invited guests gathered in front of the manor, preparing themselves to enter, Cassandra heard her name called. She swung her head toward the carriages, wondering who would have called for her.

Wearing the servants' livery of a driver, Stuart Burrell waved to her as he walked closer. The smile she had lost earlier today sprang to her face as happiness filled her. It was good to see one of the servants her father had had to let go because of his lack of funds.

She rushed toward the man she had once thought of as an older brother. "Stuart. It does my heart good to see you again." She motioned to his clothes. "And you are a driver now."

The tall, thin man with receding brown hair nodded and

grinned. "Indeed. I have come up in the world and wear fancy clothes."

She grasped his hands and squeezed. "Whom do you work for?"

"I work for a hackney company. I'm hired out to drive the gentry wherever they wish to go."

"Oh, Stuart. How wonderful for you." She released his hands and motioned toward her family's vehicle. "My family is just over there if you would like to greet them."

"I might have to do that later. The lords who paid me to drive for them this evening don't know how long they will stay, so I must be ready at all times for whenever they wish to leave."

She arched an eyebrow. "What? They are not going to stay for one of Aunt Frances's famous parties? Why, her gatherings are the talk of the Season."

"These lords do not live around this area. They are only here on holiday."

She hitched a silent breath. She knew of two lords who were on holiday in Bath. Then again, many people traveled to Bath for some relaxation from their hectic lives. Although she was positive the men in her mind wouldn't be here, she just had to ask.

"By chance, is one of these men Lord Hanover?"

Stuart's eyes widened. "Indeed, that is one of them. The other is Lord Kentwood. Do you know them?"

She laughed lightly, trying to hide the excitement rushing through her. She would see Lord Hanover again. But now that they were with *his* class of friends, would he treat her like the rest of the *ton* treated her family?

"Yes, Stuart. My family met them two days ago."

A look of concern crossed his face. "Take care, Cassandra. These men are first-class rogues and nothing less. I pray you do not get tangled in their wayward lifestyle."

She caught her breath again. *Rogues?* She had suspected as such when she first met them, and Collin had admitted that the Worthington men were all scandalous. So why wouldn't he be included in that mix? Yet the man she'd visited with briefly that unforgettable night was too kind and gentle. His only improper gesture was to give her a lavender rose. He had also rested his hand on hers, but it wasn't for very long. Could he be considered a *rogue*? Now, Lord Kentwood…she knew he was the type of man to create scandal.

"I thank you for your warning. I'll certainly be more cautious. However, I don't think they will look at me or my sister again, and certainly not amongst this crowd. I believe Olivia and I are safe from their roguish clutches."

"Cassandra, dear." Her mother's voice was loud behind her only seconds before the woman grasped Cassandra's arm. "What are you doing?"

She met her parent's worried gaze. "Mother? Do you not remember Stuart?"

Her mother's eyes widened. "Oh, heavens. It is you." She patted his hands. "It is so good to see you again."

He bowed. "And it is good to see you and your daughter."

"Come, dear." Mother handed Cassandra her mask. "We are ready to go inside now."

Cassandra gave her a nod before looking back at Stuart. "I wish you much success with your new employer, and I hope we see each other again."

"As do I." Stuart bowed again before hurrying back toward his coach.

Cassandra adjusted the gold mask trimmed with black lace over her eyes as she followed her family up the rock stairs and into the manor. She expected everyone to be wearing masks this evening, but she was certain she would recognize Lord Hanover. Yet if she did notice him, would she take Stuart's advice and keep her distance? He was a rogue, after all.

She scanned the crowded ballroom, searching for a tall man with brownish-blond, wavy hair and wide shoulders. Immediately, she saw him dancing with a woman wearing a mask with peacock feathers. A sigh escaped Cassandra's throat before she could stop it. He was devilishly handsome in his black coat and trousers, with a red-gold waistcoat and white cravat. Indeed, this was Collin Worthington. No other man could make her heartbeat skip with anxiousness. Even his mouth looked familiar.

"Cassandra, dear," her mother whispered, grasping her elbow. "You must do *all* you can to attract the attention of one of these wealthy men. I fear your father has left us in dire straits, and it is up to you to charm one of them."

Panic filled Cassandra as she stared into the shadowed slits of her mother's mask. "What are you saying?"

"I'm saying that tonight you need to target your future husband…and do what is necessary to make him offer marriage."

Do what is necessary… Cassandra's mouth turned cotton dry. Her mother couldn't possibly mean what she thought. Something like that would certainly cause a scandal. Perhaps she was overthinking. Maybe her mother just wanted her to get to know a man in hopes of his falling madly in love with her and offering marriage. But what chance did Cassandra have wearing rags and competing with ladies of quality?

She glanced toward her father, who was talking with Charles. The frown on her brother's face made her wonder if their father was giving Jacob the same kind of talk that Mother had given Cassandra.

Inwardly, she groaned. Indeed, it was up to her and Jacob to make the best out of a rotten situation. *Thanks for ruining our lives, Father!*

She took a deep breath and nodded. There was no other choice. If she wanted to get married, a scandal would be the only way. So much for her dreams of falling in love. But what if she could accomplish both? After all, she had caught the interest of one handsome lord two days ago.

Finding Collin again in this crowd wasn't difficult, since he was more muscular than most of the men at the party. What if she could get him to fall in love with her? But what if his purpose of giving her the rose while in her mother's flower garden was just to be friends? They did have something in common—their love for music. Perhaps she could use this to win him over.

And if that didn't work, she would have to create a scandal one way or another.

Cassandra watched Collin until his dancing ended with another woman. The fancy lady wore a silver gown with a pearl-beaded mask. Cassandra was certain the woman's mask alone would feed the Featherstone family for a month.

Not wanting to look too obvious, she slowly made her way toward Lord Hanover. After he had taken the woman to her family, he turned and walked toward a circle of men, stopped, and began chatting with them.

She had to stop somewhere to watch him. But, of course, she would be by herself. Then again, she was used to being at a party and not mingling, unless it was with her own family. Society shunned her family, thanks to her father's unwise gambling choices.

She kept her gaze on the couples dancing, and periodically glanced over her shoulder toward Collin. He appeared to be bored. She understood that feeling well.

A few people that she recognized passed her, and she nodded a greeting. Thankfully, they politely returned it. She prayed that those who judged her father harshly would realize that she and her siblings had nothing to do with their parent's decisions.

Several moments passed before she peeked over her shoulder again toward the circle of men. This time, she didn't see Collin. Grumbling under her breath, she glanced around the area, frantically searching for him. One way or another, she needed to get his attention. Although she was prepared to charm him the best way she knew how, she prayed he would live up to his *roguish* reputation and seduce her first.

Suddenly, someone behind her slid fingers along her bare elbow, and warm breath touched her neck.

"Meet me outside on the terrace in five minutes."

She gasped and froze. *That voice!* She knew without a doubt that the deep, very masculine voice was Collin's. He stepped past her, purposely brushing his arm against hers. He didn't look her way as he walked toward the terrace doors.

Her pulse had quickened so much that it shook through her body. Had he known it was her? Or was he expecting someone else? Then again, what other woman would show up to the masked ball wearing an outdated gown? Either way, she must meet him outside. Hopefully, he hadn't noticed her watching him. Then again, perhaps it was best if he had seen her watching him. At least he would know she was taken with him.

She wrung her black-gloved hands against her middle as she swung her attention to the people standing close to her. Nobody looked at her as if they had seen the brief contact between her and Collin. Everyone seemed to be wrapped up in their own lives. With any luck, things would remain that way.

How many minutes had passed? Perhaps she should have been counting them instead of thinking about Collin. However, she would start on her way regardless of the time. She was too anxious to wait any longer. She wanted to know why he wanted her to meet him on the terrace. At the same time, she hoped he didn't think she was someone else. Her already low self-esteem wouldn't be able to take the blow.

With each step toward the terrace doors, her heart hammered that much faster. Part of her wanted to turn away her mother's suggestion, and yet Cassandra knew this would be the only chance she had at finding a decent husband.

Pushing away the warnings ringing in her ears, she stepped outside. A few couples were strolling through her aunt's gardens, lit only by the full moon. She continued down the main path until she spotted Collin. He sat on a stone bench, learning forward as he rubbed his forehead.

She trembled anxiously as she headed in his direction, acting like she wasn't hurrying. She didn't want to seem overeager or desperate. Then again, if he knew her family's situation, as she suspected, he would know exactly how distressed she felt right now.

She slowed her steps as she rounded the rock bench. He must have heard the rustle of her gown, because he swung toward her. His mask hung in his fingers, and she dared not sigh aloud from seeing his handsome face.

"Lord Hanover," she said, hoping it didn't sound too dreamy.

He grinned. "I thought I asked you to call me Collin."

Another heavy sigh escaped her, and her body relaxed. "You did. Forgive me, Collin."

He looked over her, starting at the top of her ringlets, and down over her blue gown.

"You look very lovely tonight, Cassandra. The blue of your gown makes your eyes sparkle. The color complements you well."

Her cheeks warmed. "Thank you. I think you are very handsome, as well."

He patted the empty space on the bench next to him. "Would you like to join me?"

Nodding, she sat beside him, but not too close. She didn't want to stop looking at him, but apparently he didn't feel the same, because he stared toward her aunt's small pond not too far from them.

"I'm surprised you noticed me," she said softly.

His chest shook with a silent laugh. "It is hard to ignore a woman when she is constantly studying me."

She held her breath. *He knew?* "I…I'm sorry you saw that."

He looked at her and winked. "I'm not sorry in the least. It is quite flattering to have a lovely woman staring at me."

Heat crawled up her face, and yet she couldn't turn her head. Maybe it didn't matter, since they were partially in the shadows anyway.

"I was surprised to see you here," she said after a few uncomfortable seconds.

"Kentwood was invited, so he brought me with him."

The tone of his voice made her pause. Why did he sound like

he didn't want to be here? "Are you not enjoying yourself?"

He shrugged, and his attention fell to his hands. "I wasn't, but now…" He met her stare and smiled. "I must admit, the evening is perking up quite nicely. However"—he reached behind her head and untied her mask—"I would rather see your pretty face when I talk to you."

She chuckled, only to try to get her racing heartbeat to slow down. She held the fallen mask in her lap, grateful that her hands had something to do. "You are too kind with your compliments, Collin. One might think you are over-flattering me for a specific reason."

He arched an eyebrow. "True, one might think that, but I'm curious to know what *you* think."

Chapter Nine

CASSANDRA'S MIND TURNED blank. Really, there was only one thing that had been in her thoughts lately, and no matter how hard she tried to calm herself and act natural, the simple truth was that she wanted his attention. She wanted them to be alone. But most importantly, she wanted him to fall in love with her.

Dare she hope for the impossible?

"I think you are an expert at charming the ladies, Collin."

He laughed. "I will not lie. I have been known to charm my share of women. Does my confession shock you?"

She shook her head. "Although it should, I have heard rumors about you and your cousin."

"Is this after I told you about the Worthington men's sordid reputation?"

"I have heard a rumor recently."

He turned his body toward her and took hold of one of her hands. "Pray, what are these rumors saying about me and Kentwood?"

She moistened her throat with a hard swallow before licking her dry lips. "That you are both first-class rogues."

Slowly, he nodded. "I suppose we are."

"You *suppose*?" She laughed. "Are you trying to tell me that you don't know this fact about yourself?"

He leaned closer as his smile softened. "My dearest Cass, rogues like me do not go around bragging about our exploits, especially to fair maidens."

"If I'm not mistaken, that sounded like you were bragging."

He stroked her hand. "Tell me, Cassandra, if you know I'm a rogue, why are you out here with me?"

Oh, heavens... The truth would come out sooner than she wanted. She couldn't allow that to happen.

"Would you believe that you are the only one I know at this ball, besides my family?"

His gaze narrowed on her. "That would be very difficult to believe."

"Let me rephrase that." She took a deep breath as her mind twirled with what to say. "You are the only one who has willingly sought my company. The others here tonight turn up their noses at me and my family. We are here only because my aunt invited us."

"Your aunt?"

"Yes. Lady Frances Guthrie is my aunt."

He locked his gaze on hers as if trying to read her mind. Finally, he nodded, and realization dawned on his face.

"Then the rumors about you are true?" he asked.

She snorted a laugh. "Rumors about me? Pray, what could people have to say about me?"

"Well, actually, they are about your father."

Her heart sank and her enthusiasm vanished. The truth was finally out. "Indeed. They are true."

His fingers stroked her hand again, slower this time. "So, your father gambled away your dowry?"

"He gambled away *everything.*"

"That would be why you have no servants."

"And, of course, why he was embarrassed to mention it the other night at dinner." She shrugged. "Sadly enough, we cannot control our father. Even though he is ruining our lives."

He frowned. "I fully understand."

"Collin, is *your* father like this?"

"My father is not a gambler. However, he wants to control everyone around him, especially his sons. It irritates me, because he wasn't around much while Adrian and I were growing up and needed a father. But now, he wants to control everything we do." He glanced at their touching hands. "I don't know how to tell him to stop."

"What is he doing now?"

He lifted his focus, resting it on her face again. "He has purchased a manor for my brother and me. Father thinks we need to become responsible adults and make good choices, but mostly, he wants us to get along."

She arched an eyebrow. "You and your brother don't like each other?"

Collin's chest shook with silent laughter. "We don't agree on anything. I think he is wayward, and he thinks I'm a know-it-all."

Cassandra laughed. "That sounds like my brothers."

"But while I have been away, my father has moved my belongings to the new manor, and expects me and Adrian to live together in harmony." He shook his head. "I don't want to live with my brother, but I don't know how to tell Father to let me live my own life."

Her heart clenched. She understood him completely. "You are most fortunate that you are a man and not a woman. At least you can leave whenever you wish, whereas I cannot because I'm unwed."

He squeezed her hand lightly. "We are a similar pair, are we not? We both feel trapped and don't know what to do about it."

"That is exactly how I feel."

Silence stretched between them for the next few minutes. It was her turn to stare at the pond, but her mind wouldn't leave the incredibly handsome man sitting beside her, still caressing her hand. Now that he knew about her family, she was surprised he wasn't making up some excuse to get away from her. Most men would have done that. Perhaps Collin needed time to think about his escape first.

"Cassandra? Would you think it bold of me to ask you to take a stroll with me? The last time I asked you, we didn't get far before we were interrupted."

Her heartbeat skipped excitedly as she studied his shadowed face. He couldn't be serious, but his expression showed he was. It surprised her that he wasn't leaving her because of her father's mistakes. "I…um, no."

His eyebrows creased together. "No?"

"No, I would not think you were bold for asking."

The wrinkles in his forehead disappeared, and he chuckled. "Splendid." He stood and offered his elbow to her. She rose to her feet and hooked her hand around his elbow.

He led them away from the manor and further into Aunt Frances's gardens. Soon, they would be totally alone, but she wasn't afraid any longer. She enjoyed his company, and from what she could tell so far, he enjoyed hers as well.

It pleased her that he noticed how alike they were. Perhaps that would be the opening she needed to charm him—or the other way around. As long as someone got seduced tonight or caused a scandal, that would be reason enough for them to marry. Her father would make certain of it.

"Collin?" she asked, breaking the silence. "How long will you and Lord Kentwood be in Bath?"

"That is not determined yet. I actually came with him, and I'm not certain about his plans. Thankfully, I'm delaying my return home to my new place of residence, so I might stay a little while longer." He glanced at her. "Why do you ask?"

"I just wanted to know for how long I might get to see you before you leave."

"Will you be in Bath anytime soon?"

She shrugged. "I could be. I go to the marketplace once a week."

He chuckled. "Then I suppose I could arrange to meet you somewhere."

"I do enjoy talking to you," she said meekly.

"And you are a delight." He winked. "I enjoy our talks as well."

Excitement shot through her. Things were falling into place so perfectly. She just prayed he didn't know what was really on her mind. "I suppose I could borrow my father's horse and ride out to meet you."

He slowed his footsteps as he looked over his shoulder toward the manor. She followed his gaze. They were far enough away from the house that nobody could see them. Would that be reason enough for Collin to try to kiss her this time?

Suddenly, he made a sharp turn and headed into the thicket of trees, pulling her along. They didn't get very far before he stopped and took her in his arms. Her heart soared with happiness, but once she slid her hands up his chest and gazed into his shadowed face, the mood between them changed. The air around her sizzled with anticipation. Touching him this way made it difficult to breathe.

"Forgive me if I'm wrong," he said in a deep voice, "but I cannot help but wonder if this is what you want, too."

She licked her dry lips. "I must confess that ever since you gave me that rose, I have wondered what it would feel like to be held by such a strong man."

One of his large hands cupped the side of her face. "That is all? You only wondered what it would feel like to be *held*?"

Closing her eyes, she snuggled her cheek against his palm. "Actually, I have dared to wonder about more, but I knew it couldn't be possible."

"Why can't it be possible?" he whispered, brushing his lips across her cheek.

Her heart jumped so crazily, she could scarcely breathe. "I…I thought about kissing—"

Before she finished her sentence, his mouth covered hers. The contact was shocking, and she gasped, but the moment his tender lips moved on hers, she sighed heavily and leaned against his hard body. His hands roamed slowly up and down her back, gently pulling her closer. She clung to his shoulders, answering his heady kisses the best she could, since this was the first time a man had ever passionately kissed her.

Cassandra's head whirled faster, and her heartbeat quickened. Yet breaking away from him was the last thing she wanted. The experience was meaningful, and made her heart expand. Warmth encased her, making her hotter by the second. For a moment, she wondered if she was ill, but she didn't want to pull away to find out. Kissing him was much more enjoyable.

His mouth tore away from hers and his lips moved over her jaw and down her neck. Trickles of delight danced over her skin, and her body grew limp. Perhaps she was ill after all. Thankfully, his strong arms held her up, or she would crumple to the ground.

Suddenly, he stopped and lifted his head. She stared deep into his shadowed eyes, and her heart melted even more. Passion was etched on his expression. She was certain hers looked the same.

"My sweet Cass. I fear I may have gone too far."

Confusion filled her. *Too far?* "But we haven't moved."

His irresistible mouth stretched into a grin. "No, I mean that I should not have kissed you so passionately."

She arched an eyebrow. "Is there another way to kiss that is less exciting? Because I assure you, *passionately* is much better."

Chuckling, he pulled her closer, and she pressed her cheek against his chest. Inhaling deeply, she knew she never wanted to leave his arms, and she wanted to smell his scent of spice and musk all the time. Silently she prayed that this amazing feeling would never leave.

"Oh, my sweet Cass. I forget how innocent you are."

She loved how he shortened her name. It was so endearing. "Indeed I am, but I'm willing to learn, regardless of my inno-cence."

A groan rattled in his chest as he bent his head and captured her mouth again. Obviously, he liked her response. Very much so, in fact. The way he kissed her was so different this time. It was wilder, and the passion level had been taken up several notches. She could scarcely breathe from his sultry kisses, yet at the same time, she couldn't catch her breath fast enough.

Perhaps convincing him to become her husband wouldn't be a difficult thing to do. Her hopes lifted. How soon should she bring up the subject? She would wait until after they were finished kissing. And she prayed he was open to the marriage idea.

She snuggled against him more, releasing a satisfied sigh. But the sudden rattle of bushes brought both of them alert. They jumped apart. The absence of his hold made her sway, but she quickly adjusted her footing so she wouldn't fall.

Another man came toward them, but she couldn't quite see his face. A different rhythm took over her heartbeat. If it was her father, then he would definitely make sure Collin did the right thing by her. But would Collin hate her for it?

COLLIN TRIED TO regulate his breathing, but the panic filling him made it impossible. To be pulled so quickly out of a passionate kiss, and to realize the danger of being caught, had affected him so fast that he couldn't think straight. How could they not have been caught? Whoever this person was would certainly tell Cassandra's father about catching them alone and in a scandalous embrace.

Unless it *was* her father…

Swallowing the terror rising in his throat, he concentrated on the man coming toward them. Collin's mind was sluggish and wouldn't work properly, but he needed to come up with an excuse quickly in order to smooth over what just happened between him and his sweet, innocent Cassandra.

When the intruder was closer, Cassandra sighed and placed her hand to her neck. He glanced at her relaxed body. She smiled weakly at the unknown man.

"Oh, Stuart. It is you," she said, breathless.

Collin frowned. She knew this man and called him by his first name?

"Miss Featherstone?" The man's gaze jumped back and forth between her and Collin. "What are you doing out here so far away from the party?"

"Um, well…" she stammered.

Finally, Collin recognized the man. It was the driver of the hackney that Kentwood had hired. He stepped forward, aiming his scowl at the man. "You should not talk that way to a lady," he snapped. "The question should be…what are *you* doing here?"

"Uh, forgive me, my lord, and Miss Featherstone, but Lord Kentwood sent me to find you."

Confusion filled Collin. "You are here to find *me*?"

"Yes, my lord. He is waiting for you in the hackney."

"Then tell Lord Kentwood I will be there momentarily."

The man looked back at Cassandra, who stood stiff as she wrung her hands against her middle.

"Stuart," she said in a small voice, "please do not tell anyone you saw me out here, unchaperoned."

The man nodded. "As you wish, Miss Featherstone."

Once the driver left the area, Collin breathed a little easier. However, Cassandra still appeared very stiff. He rubbed her shoulders, trying to get her to relax.

"It will be all right," he told her.

She shrugged. "Servants like to gossip."

"How do you know my driver?"

"He once worked for my father." Her voice shook.

Collin wrapped his arms around her, urging her closer, but she pushed away from him. "Collin, we were almost caught."

"Yes, I know, and I apologize for taking advantage of the situation."

"It was not your fault entirely. I did agree to come with you, and I agreed to kiss…" Her gaze dropped to his mouth and her throat jumped. "I didn't stop you because I enjoyed it so much."

"And I enjoyed it as well."

Inwardly, he groaned. He wanted her back in his arms, kissing him with the wild abandonment that made him yearn for more. He hadn't felt that satisfied by a woman's kiss for so long, and he didn't want to stop it.

"I'm sorry you have to leave," she whispered.

"As am I."

He continued to stare at her and was happy that she didn't act like she wanted to leave, either. If only he could stay longer. Then again, if he stayed, he would be tempted to keep her outside, holding her, and kissing her to his greatest delight. However, eventually, he would want to do more, and he couldn't possibly do that to her. She was too innocent, and unmarried.

"We should leave, but not together," she said.

He caressed her cheek. "My sweet Cass, please don't worry. I'll make sure your name is not ruined."

As she stared at him, her shoulders slowly relaxed, and a smile touched her face. "Do you promise?"

"Of course." He rubbed his thumb on her cheek. "I feel the same as you do, and getting caught in a passionate embrace is definitely not something I want to happen, either. But I'll warn Stuart to keep his mouth shut. I might have to pay him off, as well."

Her smile disappeared. "Oh, I see." She moved toward the manor. "I should go now."

"Yes, and I shall keep watch to make sure you return to your aunt's house unscathed."

"I thank you."

She took a step past him, and he grasped her arm, stopping her. When her teary eyes looked up at him, his heart wrenched. He understood her fear, but he was sure she felt as he did—that their kiss had only accomplished one thing. Indeed, he needed to see her again. And soon.

"What are you doing tomorrow?"

She blinked as if dazed. "I don't really know."

"I want to see you again. Perhaps I'll call on you, or…"

"Or?"

"Or maybe we should meet someplace private."

Her smile returned, making his heart light.

"That does sound more intriguing. I'll await your message to let me know where you want to meet."

He cupped her chin. "I'll find a place that nobody will suspect. I don't want interruptions."

"Me neither."

Her pretty face brightened mere moments before she pulled away and continued moving out of the thicket of trees and toward the manor. As promised, he watched her until she was nearly at the house. Thankfully, nobody spotted her—that he could see, anyway.

With a light heart, he hurried toward the waiting coaches until he spotted the hackney. Stuart stood by the door, waiting to assist Collin inside.

He stopped in front of the driver and narrowed his gaze on the man. "Do I have your word, as a gentleman, that you will not gossip about Miss Featherstone and what you witnessed this evening?"

The driver lifted his chin and pulled his shoulders back. "She and her family are my friends. I wouldn't hurt Miss Featherstone for all the money in the world. She is a caring woman with a huge heart, and I will do anything to protect her reputation."

Collin nodded. "Then I had better not hear anything about what happened tonight."

The man's mouth tightened. "It won't be from my lips."

"Splendid." Collin opened the hackney door and climbed inside.

Kentwood sat on the bench with his face pressed against the wall of the vehicle. His eyes were closed and drool slid from his mouth. *How pathetic!*

Collin rolled his eyes. If only he could convince the man to stop drinking so much. One of these days, the drink would kill his cousin, Collin was certain of it.

Purposely, he slammed the door. Kentwood jerked to a sitting position. One side of his hair stood up higher from where it had been flattened against the vehicle's wall. He blinked as if trying to gain his bearings. When his expression registered recognition, he chuckled and relaxed back in his seat.

"Ah, Hanover. I'm glad to see you have finally come."

Stretching his legs in front of him, Collin relaxed on his seat and linked his fingers together, resting them across his middle. "I cannot believe you had the driver fetch me."

Lloyd shrugged. "I couldn't see you inside the ballroom. I figured you found a woman to seduce and had taken her out back."

"And what if I had? You could have waited, but no. You would rather interrupt my pleasurable moment by sending the driver to find me."

"There is no need to get riled. Besides, I probably did you a favor."

Collin tilted his head, shooting a scowl at his cousin. "A *favor*? Pray, how does your alcohol-addled mind think you have done me a favor?"

"Because she was trying to trap you into marriage." Kentwood tapped his fingers against his temples. "The women nowadays are cunning, I tell you. They see wealthy, titled men, and they create ways to get us into a compromising position just so their overeager fathers could find us and force us to marry the wenches."

Cassandra's pretty face popped into his mind, and he sighed with contentment. There was no way his sweet Cass would try to trap him. But she was definitely captivated with kissing him tonight, and her innocence was what had enthralled him. Yet it had been his idea to go for that stroll, not hers. That let him know she wasn't one of those calculating women his cousin was talking about.

"Well, I can assure you that entrapment wasn't on the mind of the woman I was with. It was my idea to find someplace private. It was my idea to kiss her, and it was my plan to make her sigh with passion."

"That is good to know. You are most fortunate you found someone before that Featherstone girl caught you."

Collin hitched a silent breath. If his friend said anything to degrade her in any way, Collin would toss the inebriated man out of the hackney. "Why do you think Miss Featherstone was trying to catch me?"

"Was it not obvious the other night while at her home? She is infatuated with you, and I saw her and her family at the ball. Their out-of-date gowns made them stand out, pitifully so. I almost felt sorry for them."

Gnashing his teeth, Collin sat up straighter and fisted his hands. "You should not judge them by what they wear. I found Miss Featherstone and her family to be quite charming, after I had given them a chance, of course. I'll admit, I was rather upset that our plans had gone awry that day, what with the carriage breaking down, but visiting with Miss Featherstone and her family relaxed me. I quite enjoyed myself."

Releasing a disgusted groan, Kentwood shook his head. "Oh, don't tell me she has already gotten you in her clutches. I thought you were wiser than to fall for her scheming."

Anger climbed higher inside Collin. "I will forgive you because you are foxed and do not know what you're talking about, but I warn you, you are treading on thin ice. Take my advice and close your eyes and return to your drunken dreams. You are sorely tempting my patience with this topic, and I assure you, I will win."

Kentwood stared at Collin for the longest time before shrugging and closing his eyes. "I shall let it rest, but don't come crying to me when she traps you into marriage."

Exhaling slowly, Collin tried to ease his temper. There was no reasoning with his foxed friend. By now, Collin knew how to spot a woman who was looking for a titled man with a hefty bank account. Cassandra was nothing like those other women. From what he could tell about the adorable Miss Featherstone, she was more interested in learning about passion.

Collin grinned. And he was definitely interested in becoming her teacher.

Chapter Ten

Cassandra's mind was still in a dither as she walked toward the manor. Her heart sped like an out-of-control horse, and her limbs hadn't gained strength from that very steamy kiss with Collin. Could she return to the ball feeling like this?

Inhaling slowly, she placed her hand to her bosom. How that man could take her completely out of her environment and make her feel as if she was floating on air, she didn't know. But she wanted to do it again…and again…and again.

The lights from the manor brightened the terrace, and she stopped underneath the canopy branches of the tree to compose herself, grateful that although her mind was still unclear, at least her feet had brought her back to the party.

The terrace was littered with more couples, still wearing masks. She hoped they wouldn't suspect anything when she emerged from the shadows by herself.

She licked her lips and then touched a finger to the still-swollen part of her face. Funny, how her mouth could feel this way, even though it had been several minutes since she was in Collin's arms, kissing him so passionately. But would anyone else notice her lips that had been kissed so urgently? At least they wouldn't know who she was with her mask…

She groaned, realizing she had forgotten her mask.

Cassandra spun around and headed back toward the trees

where she and Collin had hidden. She must have dropped her mask there, and without it, her secret would be exposed. Anyone who looked directly at her would know she had just left the best experience of her lonely, miserable life.

As she stepped into the alcove of trees, she held her breath, wondering if Collin would still be here, but when the area was empty, her heart sank. Of course he wouldn't still be here. His cousin wanted to leave, so why would Collin stay?

It took her longer than she had thought to find her mask. The alcove held more shadows than before. Once she placed it over her eyes again, she headed back toward the party she had never wanted to attend in the first place. If only she could convince her family to leave now, that would make her night less complicated. Knowing her father, they would stay until his eldest son or daughter had found someone to wed—or cause a scandal with.

Grumbling, she walked past the couples on the terrace and went inside the crowded ballroom. The air was stuffy, and she wanted to be outside instead. It didn't take long before she spotted her parents. They were talking with a middle-aged man she had never met. Then again, he wore a mask, so maybe she had met him before, but he didn't look familiar.

Her first instinct was to turn and go somewhere else, but then she needed to at least try to convince her parents to leave. She would complain of a headache. After all, just thinking about staying a few more hours was indeed making her head pound.

When her father noticed her, his eyes widened, and he motioned with his hand for her to come closer. Hesitantly, she complied, only because she didn't like her father's excited expression. She knew this was something she wouldn't like.

"Yes, Father?" she asked timidly.

"My dear, I would like to introduce you to the Earl of Wheatly. He is your Aunt Frances's closest neighbor." Father looked at the other man. "And this is my precious daughter, Cassandra Featherstone."

She curtsied. "It is very nice to meet you, my lord."

"You are prettier than your aunt described." He bowed and stumbled, but quickly righted himself.

Silently, she groaned. The man was completely foxed. She had no doubt her father had struck up a conversation with the man and kept the liquor coming. How else would he be able to get a man interested in her?

"Is your wife with you this evening?" Cassandra inquired, although she knew his answer.

The glassy-eyed man shook his head. "My wife died two years ago."

"Oh, my apologies, then."

Father touched her shoulder. "But the earl is searching for a wife."

I'm sure he is. She tried to smile even if she wanted to scowl. "Then I hope you find one."

Her father chuckled, and the other man joined him, which made his large belly jiggle. How she loathed this conversation, but not as much as the men involved.

"My dear," her father said, "that is why Lord Wheatly has come to make your acquaintance."

"How nice," she mumbled.

"By chance, Miss Feather...stoop," the earl stammered. "Would you like to go for a stroll out on the terrace with me?"

Did her father really expect her to marry a man who couldn't even pronounce her name? And the way his gaze wandered over her attire and how he couldn't stand up straight—she was certain he wouldn't be able to make it to the terrace without falling over. And to take a *stroll?* Indeed, the man would be on the ground unconscious before the night was over.

"Actually, I..." She couldn't accept, even if it meant her father would be upset at her for weeks. And her mother's hopeful expression didn't help, either. Cassandra would be letting down her parents, but right now, she couldn't worry about that.

She cleared her throat and met the earl's stare. She wondered if he could really see her. "Lord Wheatly, I appreciate your offer, but I need to rest a spell. My head has been pounding with a headache, and I fear I wouldn't be good company."

The man blinked as surprise washed over his face. She wondered if he had ever been turned down before, because he obviously didn't know how to react.

"Uh, I suppose I can allow you to rest." He grinned crookedly. "I shall find you in another hour and we will go then."

Her first instinct was correct. He couldn't take no for an answer.

"An hour?" Her father's voice lifted. "I'm sure my daughter will be feeling well in thirty minutes."

He made it difficult to respect him, especially right now. "If you will excuse me, I shall be resting in the powder room."

Cassandra turned and hurried away from them before hearing the man's answer. She wasn't looking forward to hearing her father's tirade when they got home. If only he had consumed as much spirits as Lord Wheatly, then maybe she would be all right.

The closer she came to the powder room, the faster her legs carried her. Once inside, she closed the door and leaned against it. Closing her eyes, she took in deep breaths, trying to calm her ire.

How was she expected to take this kind of treatment? It didn't matter if most girls her age were betrothed to men they didn't know and would never love—she couldn't do it. She would rather be a spinster. Then again, living with her father would drive her insane. The only other thing she could do was find employment as a maid or seamstress. Getting away from her parents was the only way.

Cassandra snapped open her eyes and scanned the room, looking for a way out. She moved into the adjoining room and stopped, catching her breath. Her means of escape shone like a beacon through the fog. The window would be easily accessible for those ladies thinking about fleeing unwanted proposals.

Without a second thought, she rushed to the window and opened it. Thankfully, a chair was nearby, which helped her reach the level needed. She sat on the edge and daintily swung her legs toward freedom. Although this was still the nicest gown she owned, it could be repaired if ripped.

The distance between the window and ground would not be an issue. Then again, she hadn't grown up proper, so climbing trees—and jumping out of them—was easy. Both she and her sister had gotten away with so many stunts during their adolescence that most girls would have been reprimanded for. Perhaps having no money had helped the Featherstone sisters explore more unladylike situations.

Holding her breath, she sprang from the window and landed on her feet when she hit the ground. She brushed her palms over her gown before reaching up and untying the annoying mask from her face.

She glanced around, looking to see if anyone was nearby. Thankfully, nobody gathered on this side of the manor. She prayed good fortune would stay on her side as she made her way home. The family had traveled back and forth from the manor to their humble cottage many times, and she could walk the distance in her sleep. However, because she was alone, she didn't want trouble.

Cassandra searched the ground for a large stick and picked it up. This would be her protection. If it didn't work, she had wrestled—and won—with her brothers, and knew where to punch them to have them crying like babies.

As she made her way toward the main road, she took different trails to keep her out of sight, especially as she passed the carriages. Thankfully, Stuart was driving Collin and Lord Kentwood, because if the family's former servant saw her, he would certainly try to rescue her. Stuart had always been that kind of man.

It took her another several minutes of walking before she was finally off her aunt's land. Cassandra sighed with relief. The first obstacle had been tackled. Now, if she could arrive home in one piece, she would feel like good fortune was indeed smiling upon her.

The moon was high in the sky, lighting her way. The brightness also helped her to see rodents who scurried past her on the road. They didn't bother her. Much. It was the two-legged rodents with wandering hands, a foul mouth, and who drank too much that upset her. Hopefully, Lord Wheatly wouldn't remember their introduction when he awoke tomorrow. She certainly would put him from her thoughts.

The steps she took toward home were slower now as she swung the stick back and forth. The light wind gradually turned stronger, but she would be fine. However, it was the clouds that hid the moon every so often that had her worried, especially as the air grew chilly. A storm was coming. She would be home before it started raining, she was sure.

Her mind returned to the moments in the alcove with Collin, and she sighed heavily. A smile stretched across her face, making her cheeks ache.

If she never saw him again, she would have a cherished memory to hold close to her heart. But she really hoped he would do as he told her and send her a missive tomorrow. She prayed his wayward friend wouldn't change Collin's mind about meeting up with the farmer's daughter.

These past few days seemed like a dream, and just like any dream, they would end soon. She didn't believe in happy endings, but she wanted to meet a man whom she liked and could easily talk with. She wanted that type of man to want to marry her, regardless of her family's situation. It didn't matter if that man was rich—she just wanted to be happy. Of course, she really wished that man was Collin.

The first drops of rain hit her face, and she groaned. So perhaps she wouldn't quite make it home before the rain came.

The pounding of hooves on the road ahead made her pause. All she could see was a shadow of the single rider. Even though she was nearly home, she must not let the rider see her. As if her family name wasn't ruined enough, her walking alone in the dark would be reason enough to ruin her own name. She couldn't have that.

She searched for a tree to dart behind, and at first, she couldn't find one. But if she hurried, she would reach the thick trunk and hide before the rider was upon her.

Cassandra lifted her gown and ran. When she reached the trees, she flattened her back against the trunk. Breathing heavily, she tried listening for the horse's hooves on the road, letting her know when the rider passed. But after several seconds she hadn't heard the rider, and panic settled in her chest. Had they noticed her and stopped?

The rain drizzled from the tree, faster now. Tightening her fingers around the stick, she held it against her, ready for anything. She closed her eyes, straining to hear where the rider could have gone. There were no roads he could have turned on before reaching this point, so he must be somewhere close.

The hammering of her heartbeat was too loud, so she tried holding her breath to see if it made a difference. It didn't. The seconds were passing by and still she hadn't heard anything.

Finally, a horse's snort echoed on the breeze. The rider was close. He must have spotted her.

"Cassandra?"

The voice was so near that she opened her eyes, and at the same time gasped and jumped. She swung the stick toward the man as she tried to see the person standing in the shadows. A leather-gloved hand caught the stick before it could strike her target.

"Cassandra? What are you doing?"

When the familiar voice registered in her head, she nearly fell to the ground from relief. Instead, she released the stick and sighed heavily.

"Collin? What are you doing out here?"

He chuckled. "I asked first."

"Oh, heavens." She rested her hand on the damp material of her bodice. Her heartbeat still raced in panic. "You frightened me."

"Yes, it is clear what happened, but *why* are you walking the road by yourself and in the rain?" He glanced briefly at the road before looking at her. "Did your carriage break down?"

"No. The only thing that broke down was my patience." She shrugged. "I couldn't stand to be at the ball a moment longer, especially when my father tried to force me to go with a drunken lord for a stroll on the terrace. I just…couldn't. And, of course, it wasn't raining when I left."

"Who was the man your father wanted you to be with?"

"Lord Wheatly."

Collin groaned. "Then you were wise to run. That man would have groped you and caused a scandal, and being foxed is what he does best."

"Oh, Collin." She touched his arm. "I'm so glad you don't think poorly of me for leaving."

"I would have taken you away from the situation if you hadn't left."

She grinned. "How could you, when you left with Lord Kentwood?"

Collin took her hand and pulled her away from the tree. "I did, until I realized I was wrong to leave you. That is where I was heading…until I saw you hurry behind the tree."

She giggled. "Did you know it was me?"

"Not at first. But when the clouds briefly moved away from the moon's light, I noticed a familiar gown, and the woman's long hair."

Embarrassed, she smoothed her hand over her damp hair, realizing her ringlets were gone now and her hair was straight. "I'm sorry you have to see me like this."

"I'm not sorry." He gently pulled her toward the tree. "Because now I get to be heroic and take you home. We best hurry before it rains harder."

She laughed. "Collin, I would think you were heroic whether you took me home or not."

"Why?" He stopped at the horse and lifted her up.

"Because you are that type of man."

He chuckled and mounted the horse, sitting behind her. After he situated himself on the saddle, he adjusted her to sit sideways on his lap.

Feeling his muscular thighs under her legs was something she had never expected, and a jolt of fire shot through her body. *Heavens!* This was not normal, and even though she should scold him for being improper, she enjoyed the closeness.

When he took hold of the reins, his arms circled her, and she leaned against the damp material of his overcoat. She stared up at his handsome profile and sighed. He was one very fine man.

Collin urged the horse forward as they rode toward her family's cottage. The night's cool air touched her face, and yet she wasn't as cold as she had been earlier. How could she be when Collin made her so warm? They would reach her home in a few minutes, and she wished it wouldn't be over so soon. He smelled so good, and she felt so protected against him.

She should talk to him, but no topic of conversation popped into her head. She was content to be with him like this and smell his musky scent. This moment would be stored in her memory as one she never wanted to forget.

"You must be tired," he said in a deep voice.

She shivered, but not from the cold or the wetness from the rain. He was just too much man, and she wasn't used to the excitement pumping through her. "Not really."

"Why else did you want to leave the ball by yourself?"

"Because my father—" She stopped herself from blurting out what her parents wanted her to do. She couldn't tell Collin that. He would certainly want to leave her company immediately.

"What was your father doing?"

Sighing, she looked at his face again. This time, he was watching her.

"My father doesn't realize why my aunt invites us to these parties. It is not for us to meet people. She does it to make her friends *think* she is helping her poor relations, but the truth is,

Aunt Frances hasn't lifted a finger to help us. My father doesn't see that his sister's friends laugh at us for coming to these gatherings. It is quite embarrassing, and I'm tired of it. Sadly, I have to attend, along with my family, regardless how I feel."

"I'm sorry they drag you to places like that. You know, I would rather stay inside and read a good book than attend some of the gatherings I'm invited to. But as with your father, my father expects it of me as his eldest."

She nodded. "We are so alike, and I'm grateful I have someone to share my feelings with."

"As am I." He smiled. "Do you know that Kentwood doesn't even know about my father purchasing an estate for me and my brother?"

Surprise washed over her. "He doesn't?"

Collin shook his head. "Kentwood would never understand. He was given anything he ever wanted because his parents didn't want to have to discipline him, since he was the only child."

"That is very unfortunate."

"It really is."

They rode up to her cottage, and he stopped the horse. He jumped down first, then lifted his arms up to assist her. She leaned forward and rested her hands on his strong shoulders as he gripped her waist. Slowly, he lifted her from the animal, keeping his gaze locked with hers the whole time.

Her heartbeat quickened, and he set her in front of him and didn't let go. It didn't matter if the rain was falling faster now— she was satisfied with staring at his handsome face.

"I suppose you should go inside," he said. "I would hate you to catch your death from this weather."

"Actually, I think we both need to get out of the rain." She swallowed hard. "I should be a good hostess and invite you inside for some tea, but since we will be the only two in the house, that is not proper."

He stroked his knuckles over her cheek. "I believe we stopped being proper when we went for a stroll at the party earlier. But I won't push you to do anything you don't want to do."

Heat crawled up her neck. She didn't dare tell him that he wouldn't be pushing her. "Then I shall make us some tea to warm our bellies."

"That sounds good."

"However…" She paused. "You must promise, as a gentleman, to be on your best behavior."

"Actually," he said, lowering his voice. "I'm rather hungry. Can you make me something to eat?"

She grinned. "As long as I have the food, I can make you anything."

He stepped back and motioned toward the cottage. "Then lead the way, my sweet lady."

She took his hand and hurried inside. The lamp was low on the inside table, so she turned it up. Without asking, Collin moved to the hearth and threw on some logs, then started a fire.

When he stood and looked at her, she could see his dreamy eyes better. They appeared the same after they'd kissed at the party. If she were to name his expression, she would say it was *desire*. Her mouth turned dry, but she felt the same emotion drumming through her.

They were both wet, which only meant one thing. To avoid catching their death from the cold, they needed to change out of their clothes into something warmer.

Her heart whacked crazily against her ribs. *Oh dear…* Their improper situation had just grown worse.

Chapter Eleven

COLLIN TIGHTENED THE quilt around his shoulders as he sat at the table and watched Cassandra prepare scrambled eggs. Something like this had never happened before, and he was amazed that a woman like Cassandra would capture his interest so quickly. All of the well-schooled ladies he had been with would never lower themselves to first have him strip down into his underthings and wrap a heavy quilt around his body as his clothes dried near the fire, and second to prepare his meal with their own hands. She would certainly make some man a fine wife.

Of course, if he ever married, he would expect his servants to prepare the meals, not his wife. However, it was nice to know Cassandra had a talent that most women of nobility did not possess. She was certainly one in a million.

To make their situation even worse, she had changed out of her wet clothes. However, he had been with enough women to know she wore no chemise or corset under her thin gown, and there were no stockings on her legs. When she moved closer to the hearth, the flames from the fire silhouetted her legs perfectly through the garment. His mouth watered, and all he wanted to do was hold her. He especially liked that her damp hair was straight, and hung provocatively around her shoulders. She was certainly a country girl, but he didn't mind that one bit.

If his father ever knew Collin was spending time with girl

from a penniless family, the old man would have heart palpitations. That wasn't the reason Collin wanted to be with Cassandra, but it was humorous to think that his father wouldn't approve. But Collin didn't need the old man's endorsement anyway.

"Collin, you must say something." Cassandra glanced at him over her shoulder. "The silence is unsettling."

"Forgive me." He stood from the kitchen chair, keeping the quilt around him as he moved next to her. "I suppose you can show me how to make my own eggs."

She gasped and swung toward him with wide eyes. "Absolutely not. Men like yourself should never learn to make their own food."

"Then we shall make this our little secret." He winked. "Besides, it will give us something to talk about, correct?"

She laughed. "You are incorrigible."

"I would hope so." He bumped his arm against hers. "But I really do enjoy having a secret just between us."

She turned back toward the skillet and stirred the cooking eggs. "Are you aware this isn't our only secret?"

"It's not?" he asked jokingly.

"Please, tell me you haven't forgotten about…the kiss."

Her voice softened, which made his heart beat faster. He ran his gaze over her long hair, loving how enticing it looked. Of course, she was more alluring due to the intense moment between them.

"I haven't stopped thinking about our kiss," he whispered huskily, taking a lock of her almost-dry blonde hair and rubbing it between his finger and thumb. "And I haven't stopped wanting it to happen again."

Her throat jumped in what must have been a hard swallow. She had been doing that often, he noticed. Another thing he observed was that whenever he was this close to her, she breathed deeper than normal. Then again, if she felt as he did, it was no wonder she was like this. Every time he thought of her, his pulse rate increased.

Her gaze dropped to where his hand held the quilt together, and then hopped back to his eyes. He wanted to chuckle, knowing she had gotten a glimpse of his bare chest.

"Collin…" Her voice cracked, so she cleared her throat. "You are distracting me. Tell me something about your life so that I don't burn your eggs."

He grinned and released her hair. "I think you know more about my life than Kentwood."

She glanced at him before giving the eggs her attention. "How much time do you and Lord Kentwood spend together?"

"Actually, not as much time as you probably think."

"But he is your cousin."

"My dear, I have many cousins. Kentwood invites me to go places when his other friends cannot accompany him. The reason I agreed to come to Bath with him was because he complained about having nobody to go with."

She stopped stirring and looked at him again. This time, it was longer than before. "Why did you part ways with him after you left the ball?"

He cupped the side of her face with his free hand. "Because my cousin isn't entertaining when he is inebriated. He consumed too many spirits tonight, and he wasn't thinking straight. Besides that, you are easier to stare at than he is."

She chuckled. "Can I give you some suggestions?" She turned back to stirring the eggs.

"I'll hear anything you want to tell me."

"Now, mind you, I know from experience, since I have a father and a brother whose elbows tend to bend one too many times while holding a drink."

He smiled, loving her humor. "Go on."

"The way to entertain yourself with someone who drinks too much is by having the hackney driver stop at every street and telling your foxed friend that he hasn't paid for use of the vehicle." When she looked at him again, her eyes sparkled. "Lord Kentwood would be so drunk that he won't remember giving the driver so much money."

Tilting back his head, Collin whooped with laughter. He absolutely loved her way of thinking. "And you have done this with your father and brother?"

She shrugged. "I tried it once, and it was when my father had money to give me. I pretended to pay the driver, but our servant wouldn't take the money, so I kept it. Of course, once we became destitute, I couldn't play that game any longer. But I assure you, there are other ways to entertain yourself on their account."

"Pray, please tell me. I really would love to do this with Kentwood. In fact, I could even try this with my brother, Adrian."

"Well, you wait until it is dark outside, and then you…"

Collin listened intently as she told her stories. He loved a good story, and it was more comical when a man who was way into his cups was involved. He was enthralled with her knowledge, and he suspected that being married to her would never become boring.

When the eggs were cooked, she scooped them from the skillet to a plate and gave him a fork. They both sat at the kitchen table as he ate the best scrambled eggs he had ever had. He couldn't keep his eyes off her. She was too angelic and entertaining to look away. But it was more than that, because her pretty blue eyes danced with excitement as she told her tales.

In all of her experiences, she had shared them with her siblings. For a moment, he found himself jealous that she was close to her brothers and sister, yet Collin couldn't be in the same room with his brother for more than an hour before the two of them were arguing. He wasn't certain if it was because he and Adrian were close in age, but that man had always irritated Collin.

After he was finished eating, they moved from the table to the washbasin. She began washing the dishes, and he gently pushed her aside and released some of the quilt to slide a hand into the soapy water.

"What are you doing?" she asked.

"You can't tell?" He arched an eyebrow.

"Of course I can tell. I just want to know why you think you should do the dishes."

He couldn't hold back his laugh from her shocked expression. "My sweet Cass, I have never washed a dish in my life, and I want to do so now."

She moved one step back, folding her arms. "And I suppose you want me to demonstrate how it is done?"

"Actually, all I require is that you tell me if I'm doing it incorrectly."

"If you insist."

He nodded. "Indeed I do."

She stepped back beside him as he fastened the quilt securely around his waist, not caring that she could see his completely bare chest now. Although she tried to watch his hands as he washed the plate and fork, he noticed her attention dipping quite a bit to his wide chest before lifting her attention quickly.

She smiled. "Collin, you are a natural."

"I'm glad you think so."

She took the hand towel and dried the dishes before emptying the washbasin. She handed him the towel to dry his hands, then she dried hers.

They stood staring at each other for a few awkward moments, and he supposed she was wondering what to do next, like he was. Without asking, he grasped her hand and led her to the sofa, where they sat.

"I fear," she said, her voice quivering slightly, "that I have talked too much about my family. Now it is your turn."

He shook his head. "Sadly, I have no stories to tell that can compare to yours. My brother and I were raised by a governess, and our parents rarely spent time with us. Mother took us boys on outings more than our father. She explained that Father was at work, building our inheritances."

Cassandra cocked her head. "Do you think she was being truthful?"

Collin shrugged. "I did at the time, but now I think different-ly. When my parents were together, they rarely talked to each other, and I never once saw them share any kind of affection."

Her smile dropped and she touched his arm. "I'm sorry, Collin. I didn't mean to bring up bad memories."

"They are only bad memories when I see parents together who show their love." He sighed, wishing she would touch his chest instead. "But I suppose that is what happens when two people are forced to marry when they aren't in love."

Her gaze moved slowly over his face. "Collin? Do you believe in love?"

"I want to, even though I don't have close relations who show it to one another, but some of my friends have married for love. Even some of my cousins have married for love." He paused. "Have you met the Duke of Kenbridge?"

"I have not met him, but I have heard of him."

"Trevor Worthington is a cousin. Both he and his two broth-ers married for love. They are all very happy, and, well..." He sighed heavily, looking down at the hands resting on her lap. "Sometimes I wish I had that."

"Then why don't you try to find it?"

He met her gaze again. "I suppose I'm afraid. After all, look at my parents' example."

Her smile gradually returned. "Collin, I'm sure you already know this, but we are not our parents, and we never will become them. I have seen my parents' mistakes, and I vow I will never make them. When I marry, it will not be to someone who is a gambler and likes to drink until he is sloshed. I want to marry a man who wants to take care of his family. I want to find a husband who puts me before his vices."

Collin wasn't sure if it was their talk of marriage or if it was because they were alone—or if it was because he was half-naked—but his heart grew more the longer they were together, and right now, all he wanted to do was hold her and kiss her endlessly. It pleased him that she shared his ideas of how a marriage was supposed to be, and he couldn't stop the images of what it might be like being her husband running through his head.

Leaning closer, he cupped her face with both hands as he watched her heart-shaped mouth. "My sweet Cass. Do you know how adorable you are?"

"Nobody has told me that before," she whispered.

"Then I shall never cease saying it."

He bent his head and brushed his lips across her mouth. She clutched his shoulders and closed her eyes. He gave her an open-mouthed kiss, which elicited a heavy rattle from her throat. How could he control his urges when she responded so well to his kiss and his touch?

Although he didn't consider himself a true gentleman, nor did he want to take advantage of her. He respected her, which meant he must control his yearning.

Hesitantly, she slid her palms down to his chest. Feeling her soft caress nearly had his heart jumping out of his body in excitement. A few times, he was certain he had died and gone to heaven.

Collin gathered her fully against him and deepened the kiss, which quickly turned passionate. This time was completely different than before, and he was sure it had something to do with their knowing they would not get caught. Still, her family would return soon, he was sure, which meant he couldn't let their passion spiral out of control.

He caressed her hair, but soon, that wasn't enough. He slid his hand to her neck and stroked the skin down to her collarbone. It wasn't difficult to push the gown's sleeve off her shoulder. She had the smoothest skin.

Collin broke the kiss and trailed his lips down her throat. She tilted her head back, giving him better access, which he took full advantage of as he placed kisses along her shoulder. Her moans of pleasure encouraged him to go a step further, and he tried to lower the gown a little more.

Suddenly, the clock in the hall chimed the one o'clock hour, jerking Collin out of the passionate moment. Was it really that late already? The masked ball would be winding down and guests would be going home soon, which meant…

He broke the kiss, but cupped her face until her eyes fluttered open and she looked at him.

"Forgive me for stopping, but"—he paused, trying to catch his breath—"do your parents know you left the ball?"

Cassandra's eyes widened and she gasped. Her hand flew to her mouth. "No, I didn't tell them."

He gave her a quick kiss on the lips before standing. "As much as I hate to leave, I will ride back to the party and let your parents know."

Shaking her head, she stood and grasped his hand. "They will ask you how you know I left."

He stroked her cheek. "I'll make up some believable story. I assure you, they won't doubt my word."

She sighed and smiled. "Then I shall let you leave."

He rushed to the fireplace and collected his clothes. She moved into the kitchen while he dressed. Once his boots were on, he stepped into the room and took her back into his arms.

"Don't forget, we will see each other later this evening." He kissed her briefly on the mouth.

"I'll be counting the minutes," she answered, breathless.

Dare he admit aloud that he would be counting the seconds, too?

Chapter Twelve

STANDING IN THE middle of a flock of chickens, Cassandra stared at the cloudy sky as her mind replayed every minute of her time with Collin last night. Feeding the chickens wasn't important right now. Daydreaming about the man she was falling in love with overrode everything.

Thankfully, he had somehow smoothed things over with her parents for leaving the ball without telling them. She suspected Collin had mentioned Lord Wheatly's name, because her father apologized to her for trying to hook her up with the drunken lout. She couldn't wait to see Collin again to find out what story he told her parents. Because Lord Hanover was the one to say something to her father, her parent would believe it and be honored that an earl had confronted him in the first place.

The few hours spent with that amazing man had made her realize how quickly she was falling in love with him. She hoped he felt the same. All they had shared—and *how* they shared it— made her realize he would make the perfect husband. As long as she could convince him, of course.

And he was going to meet her someplace today.

Her heart flipped with excitement as she smiled wider. She had to keep telling herself this fact, because she wouldn't believe it otherwise. However, as much as she knew he held her heart, she still must follow the original plan. If she couldn't trap Collin into marriage, her parents would find a different lord to play the part. She couldn't let that happen.

So tonight, before she got ready to meet Collin, she would tell Olivia where she was going, because knowing her sister, she would run directly to Pa and let him know. Minutes after hearing the news, Cassandra's father would search for his daughter and catch her with Collin...and insist the earl do the right thing and marry her. If good fortune was on her side, Collin wouldn't think she had any part of this plan. And she prayed to God that he would want to marry her anyway.

It had worried her last night when he admitted to not wanting to get caught while at the ball, but when he told her he would do everything to protect her reputation, she knew he would be the perfect husband. She wanted to show him that true love really did exist, since he hadn't learned it from his parents' example. Collin had a heart of gold, and he would come to love her after they were married.

Slowly, her mind came out of her dream and she heard someone calling her name. She spun around and searched the yard. The man walking toward her took long strides, wearing an earnest expression aimed directly on her.

Inwardly, she groaned. She really didn't want to talk to Stuart right now. Having him catch her with Collin was quite embarrassing, especially since the servant was the one who had warned her about Lords Hanover and Kentwood. What excuse could she give her old friend so he wouldn't think poorly of her?

"Miss Featherstone," Stuart said in a clipped tone. "I was instructed to deliver this to you."

When he handed over a letter stamped with a seal, her heart leapt. *It's from Collin!* Trying to steady her trembling hand, she broke the seal, opened the parchment, and scanned the words.

Meet me at one o'clock at the abandoned cottage on Oak Lane Road. Your ardent admirer, Collin.

Her face heated quickly, and she licked her dry lips. While her heartbeat skipped faster than before, she quickly folded the paper.

She loved how Collin had signed it. She was his devoted admirer, too.

When she met Stuart's gaze, she tried squashing the guilt rising inside her. He probably knew something, but she prayed he didn't know that Collin wanted to meet her in secret. Did Stuart know what was inside the letter? Yet it was sealed, so perhaps he didn't have a clue.

"Thank you, Stuart."

"I beg you, Cassandra, don't do this." He touched her forearm. "Being seen with Lord Hanover or his friend Lord Kentwood will ruin your reputation."

Sadness lurked in his eyes, and her gut twisted. "Stuart, do you know what is in this note?"

He shook his head. "I can only assume what has been written, and I assure you, it is not good. Being acquainted with men like that will eventually bring you heartache." He inhaled deeply. "I have known many maidens who have been ruined by lords such as these two, and I don't want to see your life ruined as well."

She wanted to inform him that this was not his business, but he had been like an older brother to her, and she didn't want to lose his friendship. Would he believe her if she told him that Collin wasn't that type of man? She knew him well enough to know he respected her and wouldn't do anything to hurt her. But if she mentioned that, Stuart would wonder how she knew, and she couldn't possibly tell him.

"Stuart." She took hold of his hand. "I know what I'm doing, so please don't fret. And everything will turn out as it should."

His frown deepened and he nodded. "But when it doesn't, do not hesitate to find me, because I will be the only one with a caring shoulder for you to cry on."

She wished her dear friend would not try to dissuade her, and she didn't know how to convince him otherwise. "Everything will be fine." She squeezed his hand. "And I promise to be careful."

He turned and walked away. Her heart wrenched. But she

knew there was nothing to worry about. Her plans were going in the direction she had hoped, and she must believe that everything else would smoothly fall into place.

Sighing heavily, she turned back toward the chickens...and then gasped when she saw Olivia standing nearby. Her sister's freckled nose was crinkled as much as her forehead. Olivia's arms were folded across her chest and her eyebrow was arched.

"May I ask what *that* was all about?" she asked.

"No, you may not." Cassandra dipped her hand into the sack of feed and sprinkled it on the ground for the chickens.

"Why was Stuart here?"

Cassandra had already planned on saying something to her sister, but she couldn't let her know now. It was too soon. "He was making a delivery."

Olivia's gaze jumped between Cassandra and the direction Stuart had gone. Cassandra knew the wheels were turning inside her sister's mind as she tried piecing the mystery together. She prayed Olivia wouldn't figure it out. There were still three more hours before she met with Collin.

"He gave you a letter," Olivia stated. "And he was hired by Lord Kentwood and Lord Hanover to drive them to the ball last night."

Cassandra clenched her teeth. Her sister was too smart sometimes. But right now was not the time to discuss this.

Suddenly, Olivia's cheeks brightened with color and her eyes widened. "Oh, Cassandra...one of the lords sent you that letter. Is it Lord Hanover? I could tell he was sweet on you when they were at our house the other day."

Cassandra turned away from her sister as her smile stretched. She didn't want Olivia to see her reaction, so she gave the chickens another handful of feed from the sack. "I'm not saying a word."

"It *was* Lord Hanover!" Olivia yanked on Cassandra's sleeve and moved to stand in front of her. "And he wants to meet you somewhere, doesn't he?"

"Don't be ridiculous, Liv." Cassandra shook her head, but her smile grew.

"I am right." Olivia grasped Cassandra's arms. Her eyes twinkled with excitement. "You *must* tell me everything."

"No, I must *not*."

"Oh, please. I'm your only sister. We share everything, and I know you are dying to tell me something."

Cassandra held back a laugh. Her sister knew her well. "Let me just say that at one o'clock this afternoon, I plan on making my dreams come true."

Olivia gasped. "What? Please, don't tell me you are *eloping*."

Cassandra rolled her eyes. "Of course not. That is too scandalous."

Olivia sighed. "Thank goodness for that. I mean, our father has ruined our family name, but if one of us were to elope, that would only make things worse."

Cassandra tapped Olivia's shoulder. "Then rest assured, I don't plan on running off to Gretna Green."

A teasing grin crossed Olivia's face. "However, you do plan on meeting the lord, correct?"

"Perhaps." Cassandra shrugged and moved past her sister.

"Where are you going to meet him?"

Cassandra kept quiet, giving her sister time to think. The chickens squawked for more food, so she tossed them another handful of feed. When Olivia gasped again, louder this time, Cassandra knew her sister had figured things out.

"Not the Griffiths' old cottage."

Cassandra peeked over her shoulder at her sister and grinned.

"Oh dear." Olivia scurried back around in front of Cassandra. "But what if you're caught?"

"Why would we get caught? The place has been abandoned for years."

Olivia's eyes narrowed suspiciously. "This isn't like you. Why would you chance fate that way? Unless... Oh dear. You are *hoping* to get caught, aren't you?"

Cassandra's cheeks grew warm. She quickly pushed past her sister again as she continued to feed the chickens. "Don't be ridiculous. Pa will never know."

"But he will." Olivia hurried beside her. "Pa always knows."

Holding her breath, Cassandra stopped and met her sister's worried gaze. Although she didn't want to tell Olivia the whole truth, her sister was correct. They shared secrets with each other all the time. Today shouldn't be any different.

She sighed and nodded. "Liv, I must tell you something, but don't judge our father too harshly."

Olivia's brows drew together. "What is it?"

"Last night at the ball, Father hinted strongly to both me and Charles that we needed to find someone that night to secure our future. Mother told me that I was to do whatever was necessary to find a husband." She shrugged. "I couldn't do that last night, but I did get to know Lord Hanover better, and I feel he is the right man. I think he likes me, so…I will give him a nudge today."

Olivia's expression grew more worried by the second. "You are going to cause a scandal, aren't you?"

"Not if I can help it. I will need your assistance."

Her sister shook her head, and the curls bounced in a fast rhythm. "No. I cannot let you do this." She blinked rapidly, but her eyes filled with tears. "I cannot go through another scandal, and neither can you."

Doubts filled Cassandra. Was she doing the right thing? What if her plans with Collin didn't go as smoothly as she hoped? Would he hate her for trying to trap him? Or worse, was he the man Stuart had warned her about? Did Collin only want to soil her and leave her?

Slowly, she inhaled the refreshing air, hoping it would clear her mind. She must not back down. Collin was the man she wanted, and if she didn't do all she could to get him, her father would find her another lord—one like Wheatly. She shivered.

She grasped her sister's hands. "Liv, stop this now. You mustn't think so negatively. Collin has feelings for me, just as I have for him. He enjoys being with me, and he respects me."

"But what if he loses that respect because you have trapped him into marriage?" A tear slid down Olivia's cheek. "Then Father will force Lord Hanover to marry you, and he will loathe you, which, in turn, will make you completely miserable."

Cassandra wished her sister would stop placing these doubts in her head. "Will you trust me? I know what I'm doing." She paused. "But I will need your help. I'm meeting Collin at one o'clock this afternoon, and after I leave, I need you to tell Father where I'm going. Just tell him that I'm meeting secretly with Lord Hanover."

Olivia nodded as her frown deepened. "I shall help, and I will pray that things work out."

"Thank you." Cassandra hugged her sister. "Being Collin's wife, I'll be able to help the family. Of course, I'm not going to give Father any money to gamble away, but I will make certain everyone has new clothes and good food to eat."

"I don't dare believe in such a miracle, but I shall try."

Cassandra kissed her sister's cheek. "I'll make it work. I promise."

Olivia turned and hurried away. Cassandra sighed heavily as relief swept through her. But there was still that niggle of doubt that something might go wrong.

She shook her head. She deserved happiness, and her family deserved to mingle with the *ton* without feeling ashamed for their father's sinful habit that had ruined them.

The next two and a half hours, she worked inside the house and constantly watched the clock. She hadn't seen Olivia since they talked while feeding the chickens. Cassandra hoped her sister didn't disappear just to avoid telling their father about the secret meeting.

Time seemed to drag. Of course, she tried not to rush through her chores, because that would make her done faster, with nothing to do but count the minutes until she saw Collin. As she cleaned, she imagined what would happen when they finally met. She couldn't wait to be in his arms, kissing him to distraction. She also hoped they would spend time talking. She'd enjoyed being with him last night and getting to know him better.

Finally, she made her way to her room, walking as calmly as she could. Well, she *tried* to look calm, but her stomach was roiling and her limbs shook from her nerves. She walked inside and closed the door, breathing a sigh of relief that her mother hadn't tried to stop her.

Cassandra stripped off her clothes and took a quick sponge bath before finding another day dress to wear. This one was baby blue, with bell-shaped sleeves, and trimmed with white lace. Although it wasn't one of her nicest gowns, Collin had mentioned how well she looked wearing blue. Since it was her favorite color anyway, she knew she had to wear it just for him.

She brushed her hair out of the coil it had been in, pulled the bulk of hair away from her face, and tied it with a ribbon that matched her dress.

As she studied her reflection in the mirror, she realized she didn't have to pinch her cheeks to bring color to her face. She was certain his compliments, as well as the memory of when they last kissed, would have her face pink most of the time anyway. Besides that, the excitement inside her would keep the blood rushing to her face.

When she left the room, she crept down the stairs, listening for sounds of her parents. As she neared the door, the only conversation she could hear was that of her brothers in the kitchen.

Cassandra opened the front door and left the house, trying not to let anyone hear her. Her heart pounded against her ribs so hard, she feared they would break. She couldn't get caught yet. Then again, if it was her father who noticed her leaving, she was certain he would let her go to Collin. After all, her father wanted her to do *anything* necessary to secure a husband.

As she moved toward the stable, she noticed the clouds were

darker than before. She prayed the storm would stay away until after she reached the cottage. Then again, with their getting wet last night, their time together had been that much better. It was almost too bad that her father hadn't caught her and Collin together last night. Indeed, she would be getting married soon if that had happened.

She saddled one of the horses before mounting and taking off. The closer she came to the abandoned cottage, the harder her body shook. Doubt tried to sneak into her mind, but she quickly ushered it out. Collin had admitted to being a rogue, but she had found a tender, caring man underneath his disguise. He would make her happy, and she would do all she could to make him feel the same way. Passion between them would be wonderful, and things couldn't get better than that. However, at the cottage, she needed him to take their steamy moment a step further than he had done last night, especially when her father found them together.

When she reached the cottage, she didn't see another horse. Perhaps she was early. Hopefully he would be coming shortly.

She tethered her horse to a tree and slowly walked into the cottage. Prickles of awareness crawled up her arms and her back, letting her know that she was not alone. Had Collin hidden his horse to be safe?

"Is someone here?" she asked in a shaky voice.

She moved from one room to the next, peeking inside. Listening closely for any sounds, she realized her ragged breaths kept her from detecting any other noise in the cottage.

"Collin? Are you here?"

After checking every room on the bottom floor, she climbed the stairs. Dust coated the banister and rubbed off on her gown. When she reached the top, she brushed off the dirt.

"Collin?" she asked again, moving toward the first bedroom.

Just as she entered, the floor squeaked. Seconds later, out of the corner of her eye, there was a flash of someone rushing toward her. She turned just as two strong hands clasped her upper arms. And when she stared into the eyes of a man who was not Collin, her heart sank. Panic tightened her chest.

"Lord Kentwood?" she gasped.

The evil glint of his eyes, and the overpowering stench of alcohol, warned her that things were not going as planned. Her mind screamed, even though no words left her mouth. She must get out of this situation...or pray that Collin quickly came to rescue her.

"Ah, Miss Featherstone. Your timing couldn't be more impeccable."

"Wh—what are you doing here?"

"I should ask *you* that question."

She wasn't about to tell him. However, she was certain he had heard her calling out Collin's name. "But I asked first."

He chuckled. "If you must know, my main purpose is to save my cousin from a fate worse than death." His fingers tightened around her upper arms. "Hanover does *not* want to be trapped into any kind of marriage, which is why I'm here. I warned him about you."

"You...*warned* him?" Her panic heightened.

"I told him not to become attached to the likes of a penniless country girl. I knew you wanted to trap him into marriage. You are just like the other women who want to sink their claws into our titles and money."

She shook her head. "No, Collin wouldn't believe that about me."

"And yet here you are, meeting him in secret—one of the best ways a maiden can lure a man into wedlock." He arched an eyebrow. "Hanover isn't ready for marriage, and as his friend, I plan on making certain he gets his wish."

Her heartbeat thundered in her ears as dread filled her. "You are talking nonsense, Lord Kentwood. I assure you, this is not what it looks—"

"Do you think Hanover is a simpleton, Miss Featherstone? Neither of us are fooled by your innocence. We saw your plan the first time we met your family." He shook his head. "Rest assured, we will not let you win."

"What…are you going to do?" After the words were out, she realized she already knew the answer.

As he dragged her toward the bed, tears stung her eyes and blurred her vision. He was stronger than she had anticipated for someone so inebriated. For the first time since she met the lords, she prayed her plans would not turn out. Being caught with Lord Kentwood would be worse than living in hell!

Chapter Thirteen

Present Day

CASSANDRA'S CHEST ACHED with the emotions she held back. Throwing accusations at Collin while he had no memory would be futile. His blank expression told her that his memory still hadn't returned. He had asked how they met, and she didn't know how to answer. And if he asked about Lloyd, she definitely didn't want to bring up that sore topic. Remembering every detail about her life since meeting Collin and Lloyd was difficult enough, and to speak about it would break her heart that much more.

"You and my...husband," she ground out, hating calling Lloyd by that title, because he had never earned it, "came to my family's house when your carriage broke down."

"How long ago was that?" Collin asked.

"About thirteen months ago."

"And I was good friends with your husband?"

She nodded as bile rose in her throat. Quickly, she cleared her throat before she was tempted to spit on him for what he had done to her. "Yes, you were cousins."

He sighed. "We must have been close, which explains how I got the title."

"Indeed."

She stared at the empty plates on the tray that Mrs. Thompson had brought in for Collin. Perhaps Cassandra should take the tray back to the kitchen. At least that would give her an excuse to leave.

"So, we have known each other for a little over a year?" Collin asked.

"Yes."

"Then I assume you are an important part of my life."

She wanted to laugh out loud, and she struggled not to smirk. "I hate to disappoint, but no, I am not an important part of your life."

"That doesn't make sense. If you aren't important to me, then how did I come to be at your estate when someone knocked me over the head?"

Feeling very uncomfortable with these questions, she stood. "That, my lord, is something I would like the answer to myself." She moved to collect the tray, but Collin touched her arm, stopping her.

"Lady Kentwood," he said. "It is not my intention to upset you, but I need to know just one more thing."

Cassandra really didn't want to tell him anything else. Remembering those days from her past had drained her, and staying with him any longer would completely make her go insane.

"What is it that you want to know?" She moved toward the tray and started stacking the dishes.

"Are we happy with our lives?"

She paused, staring at the plates. He had no right to know how unhappy she had been when his friend came to the cottage instead of Collin. It wasn't his concern that she had cried herself to sleep on her wedding night and nearly every day for weeks, knowing she should have married Collin instead of Lloyd.

Inhaling deeply, she fought back the anger and shifted her attention to him, studying his incredibly handsome face and wishing she didn't think that way. Why hadn't he realized how unhappy she was all those months? And although she had wondered if *he* was happy, she hadn't wanted to know for fear it would destroy her, heart and soul.

"My lord, I don't quite understand your question." She tried to control her irritation. "I suppose I'm happy enough now, but I cannot possibly know if you are happy."

He released a small chuckle and shook his head. "No, I mean now."

Her hands shook and the plates knocked together. The tray slipped, but she quickly righted it before everything was dumped on his lap. She carefully set it back down on the night table.

"My lord, let me get one thing perfectly clear. We are *not* together. I live here, and you do not. We are not friends," she blurted out.

His forehead creased. "We should be friends." He shrugged. "I cannot explain why, but looking at you and hearing your voice makes me calm, and I feel, deep within my heart, that we were friends once."

The rhythm of her heart quickened. *No!* She couldn't tell him. "We were when we first met, but we feel differently about each other now."

"Do we hate each other? Because I don't feel that emotion."

She forced a laugh, only because if she didn't, she would scream. "As I mentioned before, we were friends, but we lost touch after I married your cousin."

He scrubbed his chin as confusion remained on his expression. "I must have been a fool when we met, because you seem like a very kind and understanding woman. I cannot fathom why I wouldn't want to stay friends with you."

Heat exploded in her face. She wasn't sure if it was embarrassment or anger. But she had nothing to be embarrassed about, except that maybe she was acting kind, but it was only because he couldn't recall their past. "Yes, one would assume such a thing from knowing our past. However, that is not what happened. *You* didn't want that to happen."

He sighed and frowned. "Then indeed I was a fool. Will you

forgive me?"

Emotion choked her throat, and she couldn't say any more. Tears stung her eyes, but she refused to cry. Hadn't she shed enough tears for him?

She grasped the tray and hurried out of the room before he could ask anything more. It was too soon to speak after his statement. He had been a fool, but she had been the bigger fool to think she could trap him into marriage, and that he would have met her at the cottage that fateful afternoon.

She took the tray of dishes to the kitchen directly, and then wandered to the dining area. Dora had assembled most of the servants. Cassandra assumed that not all those who worked for her would come running when she called. After all, they never had before, so why should they now?

Dora saw Cassandra and stood from the dining chair, wringing her hands. "My lady, this is all—"

"It is enough," Cassandra quickly said before peering at each face. As she suspected, they still looked at her as the penniless country girl whose father had forced Lord Kentwood to do the right thing and marry her. The only thing that kept her living at the estate was that she didn't want to move back home. As she had promised her sister, Cassandra sent home money to her family, keeping them in new clothes and fed with good food. However, even though her father had crawled to her, begging for money, she knew he just wanted to gamble, and she would not pay for his habit.

"I have a few things to say to you." She swallowed hard and lifted her chin. "It has come to my attention that some of you are still spreading nasty rumors about me. But it will stop now! We have the new lord of the manor staying with us while he recovers, and during that time, you will not breathe one word of your dislike for me. Instead, you will treat me with the respect I deserve." She folded her arms. "And if you cannot do this, then I give you permission to leave and find other employment—but trust me, I will not give you letters of recommendation."

Cassandra tried to find the two maids she had caught gossiping, and they were not present. Hopefully they had already left the manor.

"If you would like to stay," she continued, "things around here are going to change, starting with your treatment of me. If you want me to treat you with respect, then I expect the same in return. But know this now—I won't hesitate to fire you if I see fit."

Most of them nodded and muttered something she couldn't understand. But it didn't matter. They had been given a warning, and she wasn't about to go back on her word.

"The next thing I need to discuss with you is the incident this morning with Lord Kentwood. As you know, my husband's cousin, Collin Worthington, has taken over the title. He came to the estate this morning to discuss estate matters, but someone hit him on the head and knocked him out. Now Lord Kentwood doesn't have much of a memory, but I'm certain it will return." She paused, trying to study each servant's expression. "If anyone witnessed what happened to Lord Kentwood this morning, please talk to me about it."

The staff nodded again, but this time she understood their mumbles, agreeing to what she had asked. She just hoped that they proved what good servants they *really* were, since she hadn't seen it yet.

She supposed it didn't matter. After all, once Collin's memory returned, and he decided he wanted to take over the manor, he would probably hire his own servants. Of course, by that time, she would be gone and living on her own, depending how much money he chose to give her. Either that or she would live with her family again. Although she didn't want to do that, it was preferable than living close to Collin.

In the year since she left her family, her brothers had found employment working for a local blacksmith. Sadly, they'd picked up the same habit their father had, and none of them were excellent card players. Cassandra felt sorry for her mother and sister and wished she could bring them here to live.

Perhaps she still would, if Collin allowed her to keep this estate once his memory returned.

As she headed down the corridor, one of the side doors opened and a servant walked inside. Seeing the man who had made her calm since she was younger, she sighed.

"Stuart," she called to him. "Could I have a word?"

"Yes, my lady."

She moved into the parlor, and he joined her. She smiled at her friend, so very grateful that he had come to work for her after Lloyd's death. If not for Stuart, her late husband's staff would have driven her away.

"I need you to do something for me." She smiled.

He bowed. "Anything, Lady Kentwood. I will always be at your beck and call."

She laughed. "Well, I certainly won't take advantage of you."

"Of course not."

"But I need you to ride to my family's cottage and deliver something to my mother. She and Olivia need money to buy new gowns. Make sure you give Mother the money, and not my father or brothers."

"Indeed." Stuart arched an eyebrow. "Your father and brothers are not to be trusted."

She moved closer and took his hands, squeezing gently. "You are a godsend."

His cheeks grew red. "Actually, my lady, you are. I thank the Lord daily for your job offer."

She moved to her writing desk, withdrew the hidden key underneath the tray, and opened the locked drawer. She kept a little money in the drawer, but didn't want the other servants to know about it.

She withdrew some money and handed it to Stuart. "Also, tell Mother and Olivia I love them and miss them."

He nodded. "I'm certain they feel the same about you."

"Thank you again."

As she watched him walk out, she frowned. She prayed Collin would be all right with her staying at the estate and living as she had been doing since Lloyd's death. She didn't know what she would do with Stuart.

But Collin she could live without.

COLLIN DARED LEAVE his bed bright and early the next morning. The throbbing in his skull had lessened, but his confused mind wouldn't let him rest another moment. Off and on throughout the night, his memories opened. He now recalled his family, and his cousin Lloyd. His heart wrenched when he thought about his dear cousin's demise. Collin had known Lloyd's drinking would eventually be the death of him, but he never suspected his cousin would drown. As lads, they'd swum several times in the pond on his father's estate. Apparently, Lloyd had been so far into his drink that he didn't think to swim to safety when the boat capsized.

Other memories made their presence as well. He remembered meeting Cass—the nickname he had called her. *My sweet Cass.* He also recalled how his heart had burst inside of him during their very first kiss in the thicket of trees during her aunt's masked ball. Cassandra had been so incredibly lovely that night wearing a deep blue and black gown and her matching mask. It had thrilled him the way she wanted to learn about passion. He recalled wanting to be the one to teach her and looking forward to the opportunity to make her melt in his arms.

Of course, by now she would have learned all of that from Lloyd. The one thing Collin did remember about his cousin was that the man loved women—and in turn, the women loved his attentions. Lloyd knew how to use his words to charm them to do his will. There were several times Collin had wished he had his cousin's talent for wooing the ladies.

He pulled on his trousers and shirt, but that was all. He knew he would be back in bed later this morning, since he still felt weak. But right now, he needed to see the manor in hopes that his memory would completely return. Yesterday, Cassandra had mentioned that this place was his now. He wished that memory would return. It seemed nobody knew why he had come during the terrible rainstorm.

As he moved down the hall, he thought about the conversation he'd had with Cassandra yesterday. Why did she say they weren't friends any longer? If only he could remember how Lloyd ended up marrying Cassandra when Collin was the one who had wanted her. In fact, Lloyd had warned him against the Featherstones' eldest daughter, even though Collin didn't believe a word his cousin had said.

The corridors were empty as he moved from one floor to the next until he reached the bottom floor. There was a music room with a shiny pianoforte, and immediately, he recalled how he loved to play. He also remembered that Cassandra shared the same love for music. Although the urge was strong to sit on the stool and play a tune, he put it aside until he had eaten something and gained more strength.

A heavenly fragrance drifted in the air. It was the scent of scones and—he inhaled deeply—ham. He smiled, happy to remember the smell of that delectable meat. His stomach rumbled, making him hungry for breakfast.

The housekeeper, Mrs. Thompson, was the first servant he saw. When she noticed him, her eyes widened, and she hitched a breath.

"My lord, you should not be up." She hurried to him as though to help him, but apparently changed her mind, because her hands dropped to her sides.

He lifted his hand to stop her from coming any closer. "I feel well enough to be up, I assure you. However, I am quite hungry."

"I shall fix you a tray and bring it right up to your room."

He shook his head. "I would like to eat right here in the dining room." He pulled out a chair and sat.

"As you wish, my lord." The older woman turned around and hurried into the kitchen, causing the brownish-gray bun at the back of her head to bounce.

He didn't have to wait long before his breakfast was in front of him and he was filling his belly with the delicious food. As he ate, he glanced around the room and out into the hall. Nothing looked remotely familiar, which told him that he probably hadn't visited his cousin when he lived here, or that Cass had redecorated the manor.

My sweet Cass... He sighed heavily and frowned. What had happened to them? The last thing he remembered was leaving her house to return to the ball early that morning. They had gotten to know each other, and he left with his heart full of emotion. When he arrived at the party and found her father, Collin explained to the baron that Lord Wheatly had been forceful, and Cassandra slapped his face and left the manor, walking home. Collin told her father that he took her home and then returned to the party to let him know what had happened. The baron was very grateful for Collin's help and thanked him profusely, and invited him back to their home any time he liked. Although he had wanted to return, he didn't know what his cousin had planned for them.

After that, Collin's mind clouded over, not allowing him to think of any more. The throbbing in his skull became more painful. As soon as he finished eating, he would return upstairs to the room and sleep. Hopefully, tomorrow would be better.

He gently touched his bandaged head. If only he could remember that part of his life sooner rather than later. He couldn't stand not knowing why Cassandra appeared so heartbroken when she looked at him. Of course, she hid her pain with an upset expression, but he could see it in her eyes that she was hurting.

Was this really all his fault, as she had implied? What could possibly make him not want to marry her when he had such strong feelings for her in such a small amount of time? They had even spoken about marriage while alone at her cottage, and his heart had nearly jumped right out of his chest with excitement. What could have possibly happened that his mind wasn't letting him remember?

Mrs. Thompson entered the dining room again, carrying the tea tray. She placed the kettle on the table, followed by the cup and saucer.

"Would you like some tea, my lord?"

"Yes, thank you."

As she poured, she peeked at him a few times, and as she handed him the cup, her smile grew wider.

"I must say, Lord Kentwood, that the staff here is very happy you are doing better today. And we hope you plan on staying here longer, but we know you have a busy life and will be leaving us soon."

Confusion filled his head. Why did it sound like a compliment followed by a polite invitation to leave? "I appreciate that, Mrs. Thompson. Regardless of whether I have a busy life or not, I would like to stay longer and recuperate from my injury."

Her cheery smile wavered slightly. "You are most welcome to stay longer, if that is your wish. Most of us remember you when you came to visit your cousin. Of course, that was several years ago. You were much younger."

Her words surprised him. "Then I take it I have been here before?"

"Indeed, my lord."

He sighed with relief. "I hope to remember those days soon, because for now, nothing looks familiar."

"I'm sure your memory will return quickly."

She left the room, and it made his heart glad to know these people welcomed him. But there was one heart he needed to change. Cassandra's. Whatever he had done to her, he would fix it. He must use his heart to guide his actions, since he still felt the attraction between them now as if it had just happened. He must do something to soften her heart toward him so that she could love him again. Being friends would not do. Not after what they had experienced together.

Within minutes, Mrs. Thompson carried in another tray. This time, a plate of the wonderful foods he had smelled was on it, plus a few more. His hand trembled as he shoveled the food into his mouth, feeling like a man who had been starved.

When he finished eating, he left the dining room. The rumbling of thunder outside drew him to the nearest window. Dark clouds covered the sky in a thick blanket and rain fell in buckets. The wind made it appear as though the rain speared sideways from heaven.

Apparently, it had been raining like this yesterday. This was another good reason for him to stay at the manor. But even if the sun was shining high in the sky and the temperature was hotter than Hades, he still didn't want to leave until his memory returned, and until he had Cassandra gazing dreamily into his eyes like she used to.

The rhythm of the rain hitting the windows lulled him in a dreamlike daze. The wet grass and trees became blurred as his mind opened and another memory entered...

Chapter Fourteen

I N HIS MEMORY, it was a dreary day, just as this one. He was in Bath at the inn where he and Lloyd had been staying. His cousin had been suspiciously absent most of the afternoon, so Collin joined a card game with three other gentlemen in a room near the lobby. Content with his winnings, he waited for the storm to pass so he could ride out to find a secret place where he and his sweet Cass could meet to be alone. Lloyd had been strongly hinting at leaving Bath, but Collin wanted to stay longer.

From out in the main hall, the slamming of the front door jerked his attention toward the open door. Even the other men around the table turned their heads to see who was stomping toward the staircase. When the drenched figure of Kentwood passed by the room, Collin gasped in surprise.

After excusing himself from the game, he collected his winnings and quickly rushed after his cousin. Collin caught up to Lloyd as he stood in front of his room, trying to open the door. By the way Kentwood swayed, Collin could tell his cousin was foxed, yet again.

Just before Collin reached him, Lloyd stumbled and bumped his head into the door. Collin grasped his arm, keeping him upright.

"Here, let me open that for you." Collin took the key away from Kentwood and opened the door. He helped Lloyd into the room and to his bed. Kentwood fell on his mattress and groaned.

"Where have you been, my good man?" Collin shook his head. "From the looks of you, I should order a couple of maids to bring you up some hot water for a bath."

Lloyd blinked his eyes open and peered at Collin. A frown was affixed to his face instead of his usual carefree grin.

"It is the least you could do for me," Lloyd grumbled.

Taken back by his cousin's ungrateful attitude, Collin arched an eyebrow. "And pray, what else do you wish me to do for you?"

Lloyd flipped his hand in a dismissive wave. "I suppose it is too late, anyway. As much as I would like to redo the last few hours, what is done is done."

Kentwood rolled off the bed, and thankfully was able to stand by himself. He shrugged out of his wet overcoat before removing his equally drenched suit coat and cravat.

Collin shook his head. "Kentwood, if you weren't so intoxicated, I would punch you in the nose right now just for entertainment. Tell me, what in the blazes you are talking about?"

Kentwood released a low groan as he pushed his wet hair back on his head, flinging off excess water in the process. Collin wiped away the few splashes of water that landed on his face.

"I have dire news, cousin." Kentwood stood up straight... Well, as straight as he could under the circumstances.

"And what is your news?"

"I am getting married."

Collin had seen his cousin upset before, but never this miserable. "*Marriage?* Did you not tell me last night that you were never getting married?"

"Indeed I did, but that was before the wench's father caught his daughter in my arms in what one might assume was a scandalous position."

Biting his bottom lip, Collin held back a laugh. This was definitely not a laughing matter, and yet it surprised him that Kentwood—of all people—would get caught, especially since he had rambled about Cassandra trying to trap Collin. Not only that, but the man must have been so inebriated that he couldn't talk the woman's father out of the union or pay money to make the matter disappear.

"Did you try to pay the man off?"

Kentwood nodded. "Indeed I did, but the man was insistent...even to the point of threatening to have my title removed because I didn't want to do the *gentlemanly thing* by agreeing to fix my mistakes."

"Who is this man? Is he a gentleman himself?"

Kentwood rolled his eyes. "He is an impoverished baron. I figured a hefty bribe would sway the man's demands. Unfortunately, he wants his daughter married instead."

Impoverished baron? Collin's gut twisted. He knew of only one man who fit that description. "Who...was the baron?"

Kentwood narrowed his glassy eyes on Collin and sneered. "Baron Featherstone. I am to wed his eldest daughter, Cassandra." His face hardened. "You can thank me once I have sobered up."

Anger rose inside Collin, pushing aside the helplessness trying to take over his heart. Growling, he marched to Kentwood and grabbed his damp shirt, shaking him roughly. "You ruined *my* Cassandra?"

Kentwood snorted a laugh. "She obviously wasn't yours, since she was willing to meet any man alone."

Collin's temper erupted and he went with his first instinct—slamming his fist into Kentwood's nose. The moment it connected, his cousin stumbled back, falling onto the bed in a motionless heap. Blood flowed from his nose, running onto the bedsheets and staining the fabric.

The fingers of helplessness closed around Collin's throat tightly as though to squeeze the life right out of him. Tears burned behind his eyes, and he rushed out of Kentwood's room and into his own suite, slamming the door behind him.

He paced his room, trying to regulate his breathing, hoping it would lessen the gripping pain in his chest. This couldn't be right. Cassandra wouldn't do that to him. She loved him! She was innocent, and while in his arms last night as they kissed each other passionately, she had shown him her feelings without actually saying the words.

Collin stopped in front of the window and threaded his fingers through his hair, trying to squeeze out the pain throbbing through his head. How had he allowed this to happen? And how had Kentwood ended up in a cottage with Cassandra...and in an intimate embrace?

A knot of emotion clogged his throat, and he swallowed hard to remove it. As much as he wanted to deny it, there was no way Collin could have her now. He would have to bravely pick up the pieces of his shattered heart and leave this place. Watching the woman he was falling in love with marry someone else would kill him for sure.

INHALING A RAGGED breath, Collin moved away from the window and found a chair to sit. The memory had brought too much heartache, and he wasn't prepared for the exhaustion taking over his body.

His so-called friend *knew* Collin was falling for Cassandra, and yet Kentwood still enticed her to an unknown cottage, where they had been caught. The pain of being betrayed twice was too much to bear. And yet... Why was she acting as though *he* was the one who had broken her heart? Indeed, there was still part of the past that he didn't know.

He sighed and rubbed his forehead. She might want him to leave the manor, but he would stay here until he discovered the truth and put the past to rest.

He found the strength to finish his journey up toward the room. Just before reaching the door, he stumbled, falling against the wall. Closing his eyes, he willed the dizziness and the pain ripping through his heart to leave.

Behind him, a woman gasped loudly. Seconds later, he felt her grasping his arm, lifting it over her head, and pressing against him. Cassandra's flowery fragrance enveloped him, making his mind want to return to happier times.

"Collin, put your weight against mine and I shall help you inside," she said.

The softness of her voice was too much to bear, and he wanted to cry. But no. Men didn't cry, especially not twice for the same woman. However, he did as instructed while she helped him stand. He opened his eyes, but didn't dare look at her, afraid he might accuse her of using him and trampling his heart. If she had wanted Kentwood all that time, why had she spent time with him and kissed *him* so passionately?

Uncertainty continued to spread over him. Why did he feel like his life was in a puzzle and there were several pieces missing? Had he remembered everything correctly? Yet nothing made sense, especially the tingling inside him as leaned against her, experiencing the heady touch of her hands—one on his back, and one on his chest. They had touched each other so personally that night he was at her home while her family were still at the masked ball. Why did his feeling seem so real when it happened so long ago?

Slowly, they walked toward the bed. As soon as they reached the mattress, he fell against the softness, closing his eyes again.

"Oh dear." Her gasp was louder this time. "Collin, why couldn't you have stayed down? Your head is bleeding again."

"I thought...I was stronger." He wasn't certain which hurt more—his head or his heart.

"Dora?" Cassandra called out. "Come quickly."

The padding of feet on the tile floor echoed in the hall, and moments later, the housekeeper rushed in his room and stopped suddenly. Her eyes widened and her hand flew to her mouth.

"Dora, I need more bandages," Cassandra instructed her.

"Yes, my lady."

Once the housekeeper was out of the room, he shifted his focus to the woman standing over him, unwrapping his bandages. Was she the same woman he had begun to love over a year ago? Or had Lloyd changed her?

Groaning, Collin closed his eyes again, fighting against the anger and betrayal raging through his mind and heart. The food in his stomach threatened upheaval. He must stop fighting the dizziness trying to take over. It was probably better for him if he didn't think of what had happened between his cousin and Cassandra. However, he needed to know. Perhaps that would make his confusion leave.

"Cassandra," he whispered as he lifted his hand and touched her arm.

She stopped unraveling his bandage and met his stare. "What is it? Are you in a lot of pain?"

"I need to know… You must tell me…"

She frowned and held his hand. "Collin, none of my servants know who hit your head and knocked you out. But I assure you, as soon as the storm passes, I will send for the constable. We will get answers soon."

"No, not that." He breathed slower, in through the nose and out through the mouth. The dizziness grew thicker, but he wouldn't allow it to consume him yet.

"What is it, then?"

"I remembered something."

She hitched a breath. "What did you remember?"

"About…us."

"Oh dear." She swallowed noisily and sat on the edge of his bed. "What exactly did you remember?"

"I remember meeting you and kissing you at the masked ball…and afterward at your home."

Her face grew red, and she straightened her shoulders. "Is that all?"

"No." He licked his dry lips. "I mean, it was mostly all. I also remembered the day we were going to meet in secret—it was raining, much like the weather is today."

"Indeed. The storm was bad."

"And I remember when my cousin told me that…" Collin's chest tightened. How could he say the words? They were still too painful to think about, let alone talk about.

"What did Lloyd tell you?" she asked roughly.

"That your father forced him to marry you."

Her lovely expression turned sour, and she scowled. "Yes, my father forced him to do the right thing by me."

"Will you tell me…" Collin breathed slower, trying to calm his ire. "Will you tell me what happened?"

The sound of footsteps rushing toward the room had Cassandra standing and continuing to remove the dressing. The housekeeper's arms were full of bandages. "Here you are, my lady."

"Dora, please stay and assist. I can't do this by myself."

"Of course, my lady."

Closing his eyes, Collin gritted his teeth against the pain. Frustration built inside him, and he wanted to scream. She was purposely holding off on telling him what happened that terrible day. But why? After all this time had passed, why couldn't she at least tell the one man who needed to know the truth? Hadn't he waited long enough?

Apparently not, because she took her time applying ointment and then slowly placing new bandages around his head. The housekeeper stood by her mistress's side, even though he mentally willed the older lady to leave.

Weariness filled him the longer he waited, and he feared that by the time she was finished, he wouldn't be ready to hear her confession. All he could do was pray that she hadn't been the woman Kentwood warned him about. But what else could Collin think? After all, she had willingly gone to a secluded cottage to meet with his cousin, instead of waiting for Collin to meet her.

Silence filled the room, yet he couldn't bring himself to open his eyes. He moaned from the pain throbbing in his skull. Then he finally heard a noise. It sounded like a teacup clicking against a saucer. Seconds later, he smelled the fragrance of the tea and the steam from the cup as it touched his mouth.

"Drink this, my lord," Cassandra said calmly.

When the cup touched his lips, he opened up and sipped the warm liquid. The tea was what he needed, because it gradually made the shivers inside him vanish. It also made his mind close until the pain was gone.

Chapter Fifteen

CASSANDRA FORCED HERSELF to climb out of bed. She rang for her maid to help her dress and get ready for the day. Although she didn't want to check on Collin, she knew that was required of her, since he was a guest in her home.

She should have held her tongue when she spoke with him last. She *really* shouldn't have left the room after telling him something that he would most certainly question later. This morning, however, she had more courage. Last night, her body had shaken with the mere thought of what had happened a little over one year ago, and bringing up the past would be devastating.

Nor would it change the way she felt or what had happened to ruin her life. He'd confessed that he remembered something, but apparently not everything. He didn't know how all of this was his fault.

When she was satisfied with her toilette, she slowly walked to Collin's room. Her heart hammered fast, but she tried to keep the rest of her body as calm as she possibly could.

Reaching his door, she hesitated. Did she really want to go inside, knowing she had to answer questions? Unfortunately, it was better to get it over with than prolong the inevitable.

She exhaled slowly and knocked on the door. She listened for his voice on the other side but was greeted with silence. Cautiously, she opened the door and peeked inside. His bed was made and the room had been straightened. In haste, she searched for any of his items, but she couldn't see anything without stepping further inside.

Had he left? As much as she had anticipated the day he would leave, she doubted he had returned home this soon. Or had he regained all of his memory last night after she went to bed? That would explain why he'd suddenly left without saying goodbye. If he remembered what had happened, he would surely know that because of him, her life had been ruined, which was why she loathed his very presence.

"My lady." A man's voice disturbed the silence.

Gasping, she swung around. When she recognized who had sneaked upon her, she sighed and placed her hand on her throat, where her pulse was still throbbing out of control. "Stuart, I did not hear you coming."

"Forgive me for startling you, but I came to let you know that I have finished the task you sent me to do. I tried doing it yesterday, but the storm stopped me. However, earlier, there was a break, and so I took the chance to ride to your family's cottage."

She grasped his hands. The man whom she had loved as an older brother for several years smiled wide. His brown eyes twinkled. He was the only one out of all the staff who had kept her sane during these days when Lloyd's servants treated her terribly. Every day she thanked the Lord that Stuart worked for her now.

"Were my father and brothers home?"

Stuart nodded. "Your brothers were, but they were sleeping off a night of being intoxicated. Your father wasn't at home."

Cassandra rolled her eyes. Would her brothers ever learn? "So, you gave my mother the money?"

"Yes, my lady. Your mother is taken care of now, as well as your sister."

Cassandra sighed heavily as if a great weight had been lifted off her shoulders. "You don't know how happy that makes me."

He squeezed her hands gently. "Actually, I do. Your family is my family."

"That is how my mother thinks of you as well."

Three months after Lloyd's death, her father had tried to swindle money from her, and although she tried to be strong, she feared he would wear down her resistance. Then Stuart had shown up on her doorstep, inquiring about employment. She snatched him up immediately. Stuart was a dedicated servant, and she didn't want anyone else to hire him.

"Did my mother say anything about the additions to the house I paid for last month?"

Stuart's smile softened. "She was very pleased. And Olivia was delighted with her new room."

"I'm so glad." Cassandra sighed again. "Oh, Stuart. You are a gem. What would I do without you?"

He chuckled. "Now that you have made me your butler, you will never have to wonder about that. I shall always be here for you."

She pulled her hands away. "By chance, did you see if Coll...um, I mean, Lord Kentwood left the manor this morning?"

"He hasn't left." Stuart shrugged. "However, I wish he would leave soon. I see how his presence upsets you, and I want things to return to normal."

She chuckled. "Normal? Pray, I don't know the meaning of that word. Not since before *that man* entered my life."

"You will soon. I assure you, my lady." He leaned closer. "In fact"—he lowered his voice—"the stable hands have told me that they are planning something to make Lord Kentwood want to leave the estate and never return."

"They are?" Surprise washed over her. Her servants had never wanted to help her. She suspected they didn't want Collin to toss them out if he took over. "Well, it makes me feel good that they care enough about their home to help me."

Stuart winked. "You may not know this, but they care about you more than you realize."

"That is a great relief." She paused. "But do you know where

Lord Kentwood is? If he hasn't left, where is he?"

Suddenly, a sweet sound from the first floor drifted up the stairs and to her ears. Someone was playing the pianoforte. Not only that, but the tune was also very familiar, as she'd had it memorized since she was six years old. At first, she wondered if she was hearing things, because none of her servants played, but when Stuart turned his head toward the stairs, she realized he heard it as well. Who could be playing the musical instrument?

The answer smacked her right in the face. It was Collin. But did he know that was her favorite song? Had she told him? No, he wouldn't know. She didn't recall talking much about their love for music.

She spun toward the stairs and hurried down. The closer she came to the music room and the louder the music grew, the more her memories of hearing Collin play for the first time filled Cassandra's head, bringing back that feeling of peace she had sorely missed. Hearing him play the pianoforte at her parents' house that first night was probably the moment when she had started falling in love with him. And once more, her heart began to soften, even though she told the feeling to disappear.

She stopped at the doorway of the music room. His back was toward her as he sat at the pianoforte, so she leaned against the doorframe, enjoying the way he played. She recalled wishing she had his talent when she had first heard him. Even now, she wanted to play with such ease, as if the music spilled from his fingers instead of the instrument.

It surprised her that he didn't have any music in front of him, for being someone whose memory wasn't back. Then again, he'd told her last night he recalled some of his life, and clearly he remembered how to play.

He wasn't fully dressed, and she found it odd that she felt comfortable looking at him with just wearing a shirt and trousers. Another thing that unsettled her was that his sandy-blond hair hadn't been properly combed. Instead, it appeared as if he had run his fingers through those perfect waves. The memory of touching his hair returned, and her fingers itched to feel the texture once more.

What was wrong with her? She couldn't be weak around him. She must stay strong and remind herself that he was the one who had sent his cousin to the cottage to meet with her, instead of coming himself. He was the one who had wanted Lloyd to disgrace her, even though the man was quite upset that he had been caught by her father and forced to marry her.

As Collin finished the piece, she released a satisfied sigh. His back stiffened, and he swung on the stool to face her. He looked so incredibly handsome with the absence of his cravat, which showed off his throat. Was it possible he was more muscular now than a year ago?

She pulled away from the doorframe and straightened her shoulders, trying to appear more proper, even though her mind was slowly filling with inappropriate thoughts. "I see you have remembered how to play." She motioned to the pianoforte.

He nodded. "Indeed I have. I have also remembered other things."

She held her breath, afraid to ask, but as she studied his handsome face, and the way he stared at her with his soft hazel eyes— that held a touch of sadness—she wondered if she didn't already know that answer. "I suppose that is a good thing, then. Now that the storm has passed, I won't need to fetch the doctor." She glanced at the white bandage around his head, relieved to see the bleeding had stopped. "How do you feel otherwise?"

"My head doesn't hurt as much, but it is still tender." He cocked his head. "Please tell me you have learned who my assailant was."

She shook her head. "As I explained before, the rainstorm kept me from sending word to the constable, but I shall do that today."

He stood and pointed at the stool. "I would like it very much if you played something. As I recall, I was quite fond of your skills."

Her heart leapt. *He remembers!*

She really wasn't in the mood, and yet she could never turn down a request to play. As she moved toward him, their gazes locked. He didn't step back when she neared, and the rhythm of her heart intensified. She didn't want to brush against him, but it appeared that was exactly what would happen, since he stood in the same spot.

Her mouth turned dry as she scooted past him. Just as she figured, her arm bumped against his. It was a good thing she was getting ready to sit, because her legs had suddenly turned into jelly.

Please, stop thinking this way, her mind screamed. Under no circumstances could she allow him to make her the jellyfish woman she had been when they first met.

"I remember how you used to love playing," he said in a deep voice. "Please tell me the heartaches in your life have not taken that away from you."

She had to tear her gaze away from his before she lost herself in the depths of his dreamy hazel eyes. Whether today or tomorrow, she must tell him *exactly* what the heartaches in her life had taken away.

She stared at the keys as she placed her fingers over them. During the past year, she had played many times, and enjoyed every second of it. But as she was coming to the end of her mourning, and devised a plan on how she would confront Collin, she had stopped playing. Now she realized if she had continued to play, she may not have had the strength to drive to the wedding and ruin Collin's day.

"No," she whispered, moving her fingers over the keys softly. "Music has always soothed me, and I have certainly needed that often this past year."

The tune she chose was one of Mozart's slower, more dramatic pieces. As she continued with the piece, her chest tightened. This piece was absolutely lovely, but she didn't know why she had decided to play this one. Yet she couldn't stop. Her eyes burned with unshed tears, but she breathed through the emotions trying to tear her up inside.

She didn't dare look at Collin. He didn't move from her side, and it surprised her how his presence consoled her. At the end of the piece, she rested her fingers on the keys and stared at the wall in front of her. Collin still hadn't moved, and his ragged breathing sounded as uneven as her own.

Suddenly, his finger touched her earlobe. Warm sensations buzzed through every inch of her, making her wilt. This was not good. She needed to slap his hand away and tell him to never touch her again. She needed to make him realize exactly what he had done to her a little over a year ago.

"You play beautifully, my sweet Cass."

The tears she had been trying to hold back sprang forth and filled her eyes. Her throat squeezed, and she didn't dare speak for fear he would hear it in her voice.

"Just this morning," he said, "I recalled the first time I heard you play. I remember feeling as though I walked on clouds as I listened to your wonderful music. It is no different now. I always want to hear you play."

A tear slid down her cheek, but she couldn't lift her hand to wipe it away.

"When I saw the music room during my exploration of the manor yesterday, I knew I had to play the song you played that night after dinner." During his pause, his tender touch moved to her bare neck. "I think you told me it was your favorite song."

Swallowing hard, she nodded. "It was," she said in a low voice, not wanting him to know how much this topic of conversation was affecting her.

"It *was*? Is it not your favorite now?"

She wanted to tell him how playing that particular piece made her sad, so she hadn't played it since. *He* was the reason she hadn't been able to play it. But after hearing him a few minutes ago, she longed for the way she used to be.

All the heartaches she'd had to bear over the last year made her life unpleasant, and all she'd wanted to do was get back at him in any way possible. However, she was weary of playing these adolescent games. When would this anger and scorn finally leave her? She wanted to live a normal life, just as Stuart had promised she would have. She wished to be free of all the heartache and pick up the pieces of her broken heart. And maybe she might meet a man she wanted to give her whole heart to and who would return her love twofold.

As another tear slid down her cheek, she released an exhausted sigh and let her shoulders slump. She was tired of trying to pretend that she was a strong woman, when all she wanted to do was curl up in a ball and cry her eyes out. And yet that wouldn't solve anything. She had done that right before her marriage to Lloyd, and the days afterward. It hadn't changed her life in the slightest. So why cry now?

Not long after Lloyd died, and the anger boiling inside her was getting out of control, Mother had told her to stop seeking revenge on those who had wronged her. Instead, Cassandra needed to let it go and trust that God would fight her battles. It had been so long since she had attended church, but at this very moment, she wanted—more than anything—to believe that she could remove this hatred in her life. She wanted to believe God would help and make her life worth living again.

Collin moved closer, startling her, as he slid his arms around her shoulders. Her first reaction was to stiffen, but then the familiar feeling of reassurance enclosed her. She squeezed her eyes shut and gritted her teeth to stop from crying aloud, even as tears continued to run down her cheeks as if she stood outside in the rain.

"No," she said hoarsely, trying to push him away.

Collin wouldn't let her go.

She trembled, and she couldn't control it. Her body and emotions had minds of their own, and she was helpless to stop them.

Collin knelt, tightening his embrace. Although she wanted him to leave, she found herself leaning into him and pressing her face against his shoulder. His large hands cupped her head, and then slowly, he caressed her hair. She had coiled her locks this morning, but gradually, her hair fell out of the bun, which she was certain he helped. He stroked her hair, bringing her anger down until she didn't feel any animosity toward him.

"Oh, my sweet Cass." His voice was strained. "I wish I had known… I wish I could have stopped you from marrying Kentwood." He cleared his throat. "There were so many times I thought about rushing into the church where you married Lloyd, and telling everyone that I wanted you. I had wanted you from the day I heard you play the pianoforte, saw your endearing smile, and heard your angelic laugh…and I have never stopped wanting you."

Confusion filled her, and she jerked back, breaking the contact between them. She stared into his sorrowful eyes. "What are you talking about?"

Using his knuckles, he wiped away some of the tears from her cheek. "I didn't think I would be able to bear the pain of seeing you marry Kentwood. That was why I stayed away. But deep in my heart, I wanted to stop the wedding. I knew you didn't love him, and I knew with certainty he didn't care for you the way I did."

Scowling, she pushed his hand away. "If you had cared for me so much, you wouldn't have sent your cousin to the cottage in your place." Her chest filled with emotion so thick she could scarcely breathe. "If you *cared* for me, *you* would have come just as your note said you would."

His face paled and he slowly stood. Gradually, color seeped into his face as anger made its presence.

"*My* note? You thought I sent you a note?"

Her head pounded with confusion. "Of course I thought you'd send a letter."

"But why would you believe it was from me?"

"Because you had assured me you would let me know where to meet you. Then, when a letter was delivered by my distraught servant, Stuart, I opened the missive and read that you wanted to meet me in an abandoned cottage. *You* signed your name."

He shook his head. "But that cannot be right."

She wiped away another stray tear. "When Lord Kentwood arrived in your place, he told me that you believed I wanted to trap you into marriage, which was the reason you sent him to the cottage instead of coming yourself."

"What?" Collin's voice lifted as he threaded his fingers through the hair not covered by the bandage. "My cousin told you *that?*"

She trembled, but for different reasons this time. As she studied Collin's shocked impression, dread tightened her chest. Had she been wrong this whole time? *Impossible!*

"Yes. I—I can't remember everything your cousin said, but he let me know that you would not let me trap you into marriage. He said you had seen through my performance and were disgusted with me."

His chest rose and fell quickly, and his nostrils flared. His mouth stretched into a straight line. If she didn't know better, she would think Collin wanted to kill someone right now. Sadly, his cousin was already dead.

"Cassandra? *Were* you trying to trap me into marriage back then?"

Her throat constricted as the tears poured from her eyes again. "Y-yes." She lowered her gaze to her lap. "I was falling in love with you, and I thought you felt the same." She swallowed hard, wishing the knot in her throat would disappear. "While at the masked ball, Father told me to find a titled lord and do everything possible to make him ask for my hand." She looked at him again. "I didn't want any man. I wanted you, but I feared you would not want to marry me, so yes, I planned on trapping you at the cottage." Her vision blurred. "I told my sister to inform my father where I would meet you so that he could catch us together in a compromising situation. I...knew you would be upset, but I hoped that you would eventually forgive me, and that we would be the happily married couple we had discussed that night at my home."

Inhaling shakily, she wished the pain in her chest wouldn't make it so hard to breathe. She stared at the carpet, ashamed of what she had done. "But I suppose the joke was on me, because Lord Kentwood was there instead. And…my father caught us and forced him to marry me."

Several unsettling minutes passed as silence filled the room. When Collin's heavy breathing broke the stillness between them, she hesitantly looked up at him. Disappointment was written over his face now. His jaw was clenched, and his lips were thinned. He knelt in front of her, locking his gaze with hers again.

"Tell me, please. Why have you blamed me all this time?"

Her heart twisted in agony. "Because your cousin told me that you had sent him to the cottage to stop me. Lloyd told me that you never wanted to see me again, even though your note—or what I thought was your note—proved otherwise. I blamed you because I thought you should have told me yourself that you didn't want to spend time with me. You should have told me that you didn't care for me." She inhaled deeply and exhaled slowly. "That's why I was so upset. I blamed you for my miserable marriage, and yet…" She swallowed hard. "I now realize that it was all my fault for trying to trap you. I shouldn't have done it, and I apologize. But I was afraid you would leave, and I would never get to see you again."

Gradually, his face relaxed. "I'm being completely honest with you, Cassandra. I didn't write that note. When my cousin told me that he would soon be marrying the baron's daughter, it was as though my whole life crumbled before me. Kentwood tried to tell me that you were the one who lured him to the cottage, but it took me a few weeks to realize that you wouldn't have done that. I knew you were falling in love with me." He shrugged. "And I liked that you felt the same way as I did."

She sniffed back another sob, but her head throbbed with guilt. How could she have jumped to conclusions? Yet she had believed Lloyd. She hadn't known him well enough to think he would lie to her, especially since his cousin was involved with the ordeal.

She rubbed her forehead. All this time she had blamed Collin when it wasn't even his fault. And she had embarrassed him at his brother's wedding.

Humiliation washed over her in buckets. She would never be able to repair the damage that had been made from *her* misguided mistakes.

"Cassandra," Collin said, stroking her cheek. "I want—"

"No," she said, and jumped to her feet. She didn't deserve his kindness. She didn't deserve the tender way he touched her. She was an awful person, and that would never change. "I can't be here like this." Her voice broke as she rushed out of the room and down the corridor toward the stairs.

Her jumbled thoughts wouldn't rest. She needed to figure a way out of this mess. But for now, this estate was no longer her home. It was the new Lord Kentwood's. She couldn't stay here any longer, which meant... She must return home to live with her family.

At the moment, that was the only choice she had.

Chapter Sixteen

"OH, MY LADY. I fear you are making a hasty decision." Dora fidgeted and wrung her hands. "You belong here. *That man* doesn't deserve to be in your company. He should be the one to leave."

Cassandra had been crying for several hours, and it was time to stop. She couldn't do this any longer. Being away from Collin was how she would heal her shattered heart.

"It might be hasty, but I cannot stay in the manor with him. We have shared too many memories, and I want to forget."

She stared at the gowns she had previously thrown in her trunk. Breathing slower, she tried to temper the panic rising within her. She had just sent her mother some money, but now that she would be moving back into the family home, she needed more. Of course, in order to get the money she hid around the manor, she would have to leave her room, and doing that meant she would see Collin again.

"My lady." Dora knelt by the trunk and folded the gowns correctly to prepare for packing. "I fear you are not thinking correctly. Nobody at the estate wants Lord Kentwood here, so we must formulate a plan to get him to leave. We would rather work under you than that horrible man."

Cassandra found herself staring, so blinked and became aware of her surroundings again, and especially the conversation. "I appreciate your help, Dora. Lord knows you are the only servant, besides Stuart, who cares about me. But you forget that this is Lord Kentwood's property now. Not mine."

"Why would he want this small estate when he has so many others that are larger?"

A chuckle bubbled up in Cassandra's throat. "Believe me, I have thought that very thing as well, but it doesn't matter. He can do whatever he wishes, and it appears his wish is to stay here."

Of course, it didn't help that she was the one who ruined his reputation when she showed up to his brother's wedding the other day. If she had left well enough alone, perhaps Collin wouldn't have thought twice about his dead cousin's small country estate. If only she could wake up tomorrow and realize this had all been a terrible dream. Unfortunately, she had made one mistake after another. Returning home was best, even if she didn't want to live under her father's thumb.

"But mistress." Dora stood and touched Cassandra's arm. "You cannot give up. I believe that if you help us force him to leave, then the others will see you in a different light. They will respect you."

Cassandra arched an eyebrow. "Force him to leave? Pray tell, how are we to do that? He is still recovering from his injury. If the doctor were here, he would tell us that Lord Kentwood needs to stay and finish his recovery."

Dora hitched a breath, and her eyes widened. "That's it."

"What is *it*?"

"Let us send for Doctor Hadley. If the good physician thinks Lord Kentwood has healed, then he won't have any reason to stay."

Cassandra didn't want to tell her housekeeper that Collin would stay as long as she was still here, which was another reason she must leave. Today.

"Dora, I beg you, just help me pack. You can summon the doctor, but I fear it won't matter. I'm still leaving."

The housekeeper released a heavy sigh and frowned. "Will you allow me to go with you?"

Cassandra tried to smile, but it was difficult. "Until I am given a fund to manage, I cannot pay you if you go with me. My family is penniless. The only thing that has changed since I married a year ago is that I can send my mother and sister money."

Dora nodded and lowered her gaze. "I understand."

"But you can do something for me right now."

The housekeeper's focus jumped back to Cassandra. "What is that, my lady?"

"Please summon both the doctor and the constable."

The woman's expression changed to surprise. "Why the constable?"

"Don't tell me you have forgotten already." Cassandra shook her head. "The person who attacked Lord Kentwood is still out there. They need to be caught and arrested for purposely striking a lord."

"But…" The woman wrung her hands again. "What if it was an accident?"

Cassandra narrowed her eyes on Dora. "How could it be an accident? Lord Kentwood was atop his horse and was struck with a thick tree branch."

Dora shrugged. "I don't know how, but like you said, why would a servant purposely attack a lord of the realm, knowing what could happen if they were caught?"

Cassandra's curiosity heightened, and she stepped closer. "What do you know about his accident?"

"Nothing, my lady."

Because of the servant's voice lifting, Cassandra knew the woman was lying. Dora knew something, and it was up to Cassandra to find out what. But she couldn't bring suspicion to herself. She must make the housekeeper believe she didn't care.

"Fine." Cassandra flipped her hand in the air. "Please hurry and send for the doctor and constable, then you can return and help me pack."

Dora curtsied and moved toward the door. She stopped and rested her hand on the knob. "Do you think Lord Kentwood will ask about you? I mean, look at the way you ran away from the music room this morning."

Inwardly, Cassandra groaned. Of course the servants would know what happened. All of them had been too nosey for their own good.

"If he wants to see me, tell him I'm indisposed or something. Tell him I don't want any visitors for the rest of the day."

"As you wish, my lady."

After Dora left and closed the door, Cassandra frowned. Her housekeeper was possibly involved with Collin's attack. However, she didn't want to worry about it. Once the constable arrived, she would turn the matter over to him. Hopefully, the man would keep Collin busy so that she could leave without him noticing.

Fortune had never been on her side, but she prayed it would be today. He could not see her leave, because he would certainly try to stop her.

THE AFTERNOON FOR Collin was going better than this morning. Doctor Hadley had arrived to check on him. Apparently, Cassandra had sent a servant to fetch the physician and the constable. Collin had visited with the constable first, but since he couldn't tell the lawman much about what happened when he was attacked, the man excused himself to wander around the manor and interview the staff.

Collin prayed that one of the servants had information. If he couldn't have justice for the wrong that had happened a year ago, then he wanted this attacker to be arrested.

After his conversation with Cassandra in the music room, when she left in such a dither, he realized she needed time to process the truth about that terrible day when Lloyd had ruined her. Then again, Collin also needed time to think about his cousin's betrayal. That man knew Collin had feelings for Cassandra, so why—besides being drunk off his arse—did Lloyd feel it necessary to meet her in the abandoned cottage for a quick tryst?

Bitterness coated Collin's mouth. If Lloyd were still alive, Collin would wrap his fingers around the man's neck and choke the very life out of him. Then again, he was no killer. Instead, he would break every bone in Lloyd's body and perhaps even bust a few bones in his face to make women cringe when they saw him.

Thankfully, fate had taken care of Collin's cousin so that he wouldn't have to do it himself. However, knowing that didn't fix things now. Only he could repair the damage to his sweet Cass. But how?

He had heard that time healed all wounds, but Collin feared that wouldn't work this time. Time only made him more upset at his cousin, and his heart broke more for Cassandra's pain.

"Your wound is healing nicely," Doctor Hadley said.

Startled, Collin jumped and snapped his attention to the physician. He had been so wrapped up in his thoughts that he had forgotten about the other man in the room.

"That is a relief." He nodded. "I appreciate your coming out to check on me."

"I was only happy to help. You will notice I didn't rebandage your head. I think we should let the wound dry now and finish healing." The doctor stuffed his medical supplies back inside his leather bag. "I'm very glad to meet the new Lord Kentwood. You probably know that your cousin wasn't the best...um..."

Collin could have laughed at the doctor's discomfort, and under any other circumstances, he would have. "My cousin wasn't fit to have his title." He straightened his shoulders, meeting the doctor's wide eyes directly. "My cousin was a terrible person who enjoyed ruining other people's lives."

"Uh, well..." Doctor Hadley scratched his whiskery chin. "I

suppose you know him better than the rest of us, so I shall take your word for it."

"Trust me, doctor, the man was nothing but a sewer rat dressed in fine clothes." Collin could have said worse but decided to tame his language. He touched his head injury carefully. The swelling had gone down. "But I thank you for the visit."

"I was told that Lady Kentwood attended to your injury during the wicked storm."

Collin nodded. "She was very generous with her time in caring for me."

"Indeed." The plump, middle-aged man grinned. "I have always held her in high regard. More people should get to know the kind lady, but alas, she has been in mourning since right after her wedding, the poor dear."

"I met her before she married my cousin, and I must agree with you. She is one of the best women I have had the privilege to know."

Collin couldn't stop from puffing out his chest. She was a fine person, but it was her misery this past year that had formed her into the woman she was today. She was indeed very kind and giving of her time and talents. If only there were more women like her in the world, more people would be happier.

If only I could make her that happy.

"Well," the doctor said, turning toward the bedroom door, "please pass on my best wishes to Lady Kentwood."

Slowly, Collin shook his head. "Pardon me?"

The doctor's expression changed to one of puzzlement. "Well, I heard from Mrs. Thompson that Lady Kentwood was returning to her family's house to live. I mean, now that you are the new marquess and she is a widow, she cannot stay in the manor any longer."

Collin's stomach twisted. Although he had taken over the estate as their new lord, that didn't mean he would live here. And he certainly wasn't about to kick Cassandra out to return to her family. The only reason he was still here was to spend more time with her.

"Yes, well…" He took a deep breath. "That is not entirely decided. I'm quite certain that Lady Kentwood will remain here and I will leave. The only reason I came to see her the other day was to make arrangements and settle affairs created by my cousin."

The doctor's face brightened. "Oh, how lovely. I'm so happy she is staying here."

"Thank you again, Doctor Hadley." Collin tried to be polite by helping the man along. Although he wouldn't mind getting to know the physician, Collin needed to make sure Cassandra wasn't leaving. This was her home, and she deserved to be here more than him. Then again, if this place held too many horrid memories for her, he would gladly purchase her another estate.

Once the doctor was out of Collin's sight, he hurried and finished dressing, hoping he wasn't too late to stop Cassandra. Although he should have dressed completely when he had gone down to the music room this morning, his strength hadn't returned. But he found it now.

The wood popped in the fireplace, warming up the room. Today it would have been nice to just relax in the heavily cushioned chair and stare at the small flames dancing on the charcoaled log in the hearth. Of course, sharing the lazy afternoon with a lovely woman who had stolen his heart would be much better.

His mind replayed their conversation earlier. She had admitted to planning his entrapment in hopes that he would do the right thing and marry her. Back then, he would have been upset. After all, she hadn't come across as a calculating woman. But now… He sighed in sadness. He wished her plan had panned out, because then they would be together and happily in love.

Just as he finished dressing and pulling on his boots, a knock came on the door, jerking him from his thoughts.

"Who is it?" he asked, peering in that direction.

"Mrs. Thompson, my lord. I've brought you some tea."

"Come in." He stood and smoothed his palms down his waistcoat.

The housekeeper entered carrying the tea service on a tray and placed it on the small table next to him. She poured a cup and handed it to him.

"I must say, my lord, you are looking so much better this afternoon. I'm happy that the doctor removed that bandage around your head."

"Yes. I'm happy as well."

She glanced at the hearth. "Would you like me to toss in another log?"

"No. That won't be necessary. However, will you tell me if Cass…um, Lady Kentwood has left?"

The woman's eyes widened. "Left, my lord?"

"Yes. The doctor heard that she was preparing to return to her family's place of residence."

She shrugged. "Well, she hasn't left yet, but she is planning on it."

"Why?" he asked in a strained voice.

The housekeeper shook her head. "You don't know?"

His patience was wearing thin. "If I knew, I wouldn't have asked."

The woman's gaze turned dark, and her lips pursed. "Lady Kentwood cannot be in the same residence with you, which I'm sure you realize. Since it is obvious that you want to take over the estate—"

"You think it's *obvious*?" He shook his head. "Please enlighten me to how it is obvious?"

She twisted her hands against her large bosom. "Because you are still here. You helped yourself to the music room this morning and to the pianoforte. I suppose that is why I think it's obvious you want to take over the estate."

Sometimes, servants could be so obtuse. "Mrs. Thompson, I'm sure you are aware that there was a fierce rainstorm these past few days, not to mention I have a head injury, correct?"

"Well, of course, my lord."

"So, tell me, how was I supposed to leave before now?"

Her gaze ran over his attire. "Are you leaving now, then?"

She appeared elated to think he wouldn't stay at the estate any longer. He hated to disappoint her. Well, maybe *hate* was not the right word.

"I do not plan on staying much longer. However, I need to speak to your mistress."

"Oh no, my lord. Lady Kentwood instructed me that she is not receiving visitors."

Inhaling deeply, he tried to control his frustration. "Mrs. Thompson, I believe you have misunderstood. I am not requesting. I'm demanding to see her." He released his breath. "Please inform Lady Kentwood that she can meet with me at her earliest convenience—as long as it is in the next thirty minutes."

The housekeeper lifted a chin stubbornly. "Of course, my lord."

The woman wasn't secret about her dislike for him. As she huffed out of the room, Collin fisted his hands. What was wrong with these insubordinate servants? Didn't they know their place in a household? Hadn't Lloyd taught them...

His thoughts stopped. They hadn't been Lloyd's servants for a year now, and Cassandra's family hadn't enough money to keep servants for several years.

He groaned. She wouldn't know how to train the staff to do her bidding, or to respect her. Before his memory had returned, he had listened to some of the servants outside the bedroom, and from their tone of voice, they didn't think of Cassandra as the lady of the house. Instead, they acted as though she was just like them because of how she was raised.

He flexed his hands. He would stay for a few more days, if only to get these servants doing what they were being paid to do. Either that, or they would be finding other employment soon. Cassandra should not be treated in such a way ever again, and he would see to it personally.

Chapter Seventeen

COLLIN STRAIGHTENED HIS cravat and slipped on his overcoat. Now that he was fully clothed and presentable, it was time to leave the room and wait for Cassandra to join him. He suspected she would finally find him in twenty-nine minutes. Perhaps even with two seconds to go before reaching the exact thirty minutes.

As he walked out of his room, he heard a man's voice down the corridor, talking to the housekeeper. Collin walked closer to the stairs. When Mrs. Thompson saw him, she gasped and turned. Her departure down the stairs was comical, but he wasn't in the mood to laugh.

The servant who had been talking to the housekeeper looked toward Collin. The man wore the finer attire usually worn by butlers. Immediately, Collin recognized him as the driver Kentwood had hired when they were in Bath a year ago.

"My lord." Stuart bowed slightly. "I hope you will forgive me for interrupting Mrs. Thompson."

Collin nodded and stepped closer. "It is good to see you again, Stuart. However, I'm surprised you work here."

The man smiled. "I'm good friends with Lady Kentwood. I worked for her family when she was younger, and she has appointed me her butler. Lately, I have made it my business to protect her. She has had a hard life."

"Yes, I understand, and I commend you for being such a loyal friend."

Stuart squared his shoulders and lifted his chin proudly. "I wanted to introduce myself to you and see if there is anything you need. Thompson tells me that you will be making this estate your home."

Home? Pray, how could he stay here knowing that his sweet Cass wanted to leave? And even if he did want to make this his residence over the estate he shared with his brother, Collin couldn't possibly displace her. But he understood her worry. Thanks to his cousin's death, this land and estate was now his. Cassandra was at his mercy until other provisions could be made. Or...

Collin could marry her.

Suddenly, he was hit with a feeling he hadn't expected. A familiar feeling that he had experienced the night of the masked ball, when he realized he was falling in love with Cassandra. Confusion filled him, especially when he had just been stewing over the fact that she had wanted to trap him into marriage right after they first met. But he didn't blame her. Circumstances such as she was in at the time had made her desperate. And being the eldest, she'd had to do as her father suggested.

Closing his eyes, Collin rubbed his forehead. *What am I thinking?* He couldn't marry her, could he? Yet his thoughts were clearer now than they had been since before losing his memory.

When Lloyd had told him about the marriage, Collin thought he would die from the pain piercing his heart. He had traveled around the world after that, hoping to get her out of his mind and heart. It hadn't happened. He had even tried to fall in love again, but none of the women were his sweet Cass. He'd only wanted one woman—the one he couldn't have. But now...what if he *could* have her? Would she want him now that he had told her his cousin was to blame, and not Collin?

"My lord?" Stuart asked.

Collin looked at the butler, trying to remember what the man had asked him. "Um, yes. I shall only be staying here during my recovery. Once I'm fully healed, I don't know where I will go."

The man's expression hardened into malice. Then again, Stuart was friends with Cassandra's family, so perhaps he just wanted to protect her from men like Collin. However, the servant had no clue what misery Collin had suffered as well during this past year.

"Is that all, Stuart? Or do you have more questions for me?"

"No, my lord. I...I just wanted you to know I'm here if you need me."

"Thank you. I shall remember that."

The butler spun around toward the stairs, but he stood still with his hands flexing by his sides. His torso moved with the deepness of his breaths. In seconds, he squared his shoulders and turned back to face Collin.

"Forgive me, my lord." He took a step closer. "But you must understand how much I care about Lady Kentwood and her family. I know how miserable she was when the wrong man showed up at the cottage and she was forced to marry Lord Kentwood. I also know that a year ago, when I worked for you and Lord Kentwood, you were womanizers." Stuart paused, inhaling deeply. "I do *not* want to see her hurt again. Do you understand me?"

Collin narrowed his eyes on the servant, feeling irritation rising inside. He had never experienced a servant talking to him in such a way, and within a few minutes, he'd had *two* believe they could voice their opinion in such a way. He wasn't going to allow this treatment any longer. Not from the housekeeper, and certainly not from the butler, whether he was Cassandra's friend or not.

"Are you threatening me?" Collin asked in clipped tones.

The man lifted his chin slightly higher. "Once again, forgive me, my lord, but if you plan on hurting her again, then this is indeed a threat. She was in misery before, and I shan't see her go through this again."

Collin folded his arms across his chest and moved closer to the butler, who arrogantly stood his ground. "Stuart, I don't plan on hurting her. If you must know, I also care about Lady Kentwood." He arched an eyebrow. "As I'm sure you well remember, since you were the one who caught us together in the thicket of trees the night of her aunt's masked ball."

"I do remember, my lord. However, she does not feel that way about you any longer. I beg you, please leave her to live this life without the painful memory of how you left her to wed your cousin."

"Whether you want—or need—to know this, Stuart, I also had painful memories this past year, so I understand Lady Kentwood completely. Not only did my so-called friend compromise Cassandra, but Lloyd also tricked me. *He* was the one who sent the note, not I."

"But…Lord Kentwood gave the note to me, stating that you wanted me to take it to her."

Once again, Collin wished his cousin was alive right now, only so he could take his frustrations out on the idiotic drunken fool. "I suppose we can add *lying* to the list of sins my cousin committed when he was alive. However, that is all in the past. I'm telling you, I did not send it. I wanted to meet her in secret, but the rainstorm stopped me."

"Yet the storm didn't stop the other lord." Stuart arched an eyebrow in judgment. "Either way, you broke her heart. You should leave this place and never see her again. That is the only way she can be happy."

The longer he argued with the butler, the more irate Collin became. "I think differently. I believe that the only way either of us will be able to put our painful memories to rest is for us to follow our hearts. She was falling in love with me back then, just as I was coming to love her."

"She will never have you," Stuart snapped. "Not now."

Anger rose inside Collin, and although he felt like punching the insolent man in the face, the throbbing pain in his head told him to let the matter rest. Stuart was only trying to defend Cassandra, which was what Collin would do if roles were reversed.

His thoughts crashed to a halt. Did this mean Stuart was in love with her too?

The realization made Collin hitch a breath. Stuart was most definitely in love with her. Cassandra was a sweet woman with the kindest heart, or at least she had been that way. Collin knew he would be able to bring out her good traits again if given a chance.

He rubbed his forehead. "Stuart, I do understand how you feel, but rest assured, I don't want to hurt her any more. I want to repair the damage between us the best way I know how."

Stuart grumbled underneath his breath, spun back around, and flew down the stairs. Although Collin was relieved to have the pointless argument stopped, his mind began to open. The man's departure seemed very familiar. The color of his brown hair, and especially the bald spot on the back of his head. The dark blue of the butler's uniform also seemed very memorable.

In a flash, Collin's mind completely opened. He was hiding behind a tree as he watched Cassandra exit her carriage after he had followed her when she came uninvited to his brother's wedding. Someone hit him on the head with a thick tree branch. Before losing consciousness, Collin glanced behind him to see a man running away—a man who had a bald spot on the back of his head.

Growling, Collin hurried after the butler. Anger fueled his every step. He would get to the bottom of this. Clearly, the servant was not happy that Collin had taken over Lloyd's estate, or that Collin was still here.

Stopping at the bottom of the stairs, he listened intently. Where had that man gone? *Cassandra!* Oh, of course. Stuart would go straight to the lady of the house and try to make her side with him instead of Collin.

He quickened his step and raced toward the parlor, hoping

she was there waiting for him. When she wasn't, he rushed to the music room. It was empty as well.

He stopped to catch his breath as he tried recalling where every room was located. Cassandra's bedchamber was probably toward the east of the manor, but on the second level, just as his room. Yet the servant had run the other way.

Floating through the air was Cassandra's magical, angelic voice. He followed the sound, and it led him to the dining room. She stood talking to one of the kitchen maids. He stopped again, not wanting to interrupt.

Although she hadn't been raised as the other ladies of the *ton*, Cassandra was, to him, the very essence of a marchioness. The lift of her chin, the way she squared her shoulders, and the way she spoke made him proud. Her very presence took his breath away.

She wore a different gown than earlier. It appeared that she wore a traveling dress. She was probably as determined to leave as he was determined to keep her with him.

When Cassandra looked his way, she paused in mid-sentence. After a few silent moments, she turned to the maid and motioned for the girl to leave. The maid curtsied and left.

"Forgive me," he began. "I didn't mean to interrupt, but I do have something very important to tell you—something that I just remembered."

Slowly, she moved toward him, clasping her hands to her waist. "The way my housekeeper explained your conversation, she made it sound like you *demanded* to see me." She glanced at the grandfather clock against the nearest wall. "I was here on time, but you, my lord, are ten minutes late."

Heavens, he had missed her spunky personality, even though he was certain she tried to act stubborn at the moment.

"I will admit, I instructed your servant in a demanding voice, but it was only because I could not tolerate the way she spoke to me. Your servants need to learn respect, and quickly."

She stared at him as if bored with the topic. "What was it you wanted to tell me?"

"I remembered something."

"But I thought your memory had returned. What could you have possibly remembered now that you had not earlier?"

He glanced up and down the hall. "Where is your butler?"

"Stuart?"

"Yes."

She shrugged and gracefully walked toward the parlor. "I don't know. Why do you ask?"

He moved closer and lowered his voice. "He was the one who whacked me over the head with the branch."

Gasping, she stopped. "Impossible! Why would you accuse him of such a thing?"

Collin took her hand, led her into the parlor, and closed the door. "Tell me, who on the estate wears a dark blue suit for his uniform and has a bald spot on the back of his head?"

Color left her face. "Stuart is the only one."

"Right after I was hit in the head and before I blacked out, I saw a man hurrying away from me with the description I just gave you."

She shook her head. "That makes no sense. Why would Stuart do that to you? He knew who you were, and he would have recognized you even if you were on your horse. And if, by chance, he didn't recognize you, he would have told me that he ensnared an intruder on my lands."

"I'm certain he knew I was *not* an intruder, Cassandra. I suspect he doesn't want me around because he is in love with you."

She stared at him in stunned silence, but seconds later, she chuckled. "Don't be ridiculous. Stuart is not in love with me. I'm sure he loves me, but only as a little sister."

"I know that's what he wants you to believe, but I spoke with him not more than ten minutes ago, and I assure you, he is in love with you. He is obsessed with protecting you, even if he tried to make me think it was because he is loyal to your family. I understand completely about having dedicated servants, but Stuart has gone beyond what a servant would do for his employer. He spoke to me like a jealous lover and not a servant."

Sadness filled her expression. "But I would think he knew that I could never love him that way. He cannot be in love with me. I refuse to believe it," she said softly. "I have been a widow for a year, and not once has he shown more affection than necessary. One would think that if Stuart loved me in that manner, he would have made some kind of overture."

Sighing, Collin ran his hand across his hair, gently touching the spot on his head that was still tender. "Maybe he was following the rules of mourning." He shrugged. "I cannot say, but what I do know is the feeling I received after talking to him upstairs. He gave me the distinct impression that he had strong feelings for you."

Tears slowly filled her eyes, and she turned and walked toward the window. She parted the curtains.

Collin's chest clenched. She appeared so sad even now. Wouldn't this kind of information make her angry? And yet…

He sucked in a breath. Had he misunderstood her this whole time? Could she possibly be in love with Stuart instead?

A pain like none other pierced Collin's chest, making it difficult to breathe. The tightness in his throat made it strenuous to even swallow. He prayed he wasn't right. He didn't want to believe Stuart was correct when he told Collin that the love Cassandra had for him was gone.

Chapter Eighteen

STUART LOVES ME?

Cassandra's mind cleared, and she recalled all the kindness Stuart had shown her over the years, especially since she had taken him on as her butler. It seemed impossible. But perhaps Collin was correct. Why hadn't she wondered about the special gleam in Stuart's eyes when he talked to her? Or the gentle way he touched her arm or hand while trying to give comfort on her worst days?

None of that explained why he would purposely hit Collin in the head so hard. A blow like that could have killed him. Never in her life had she known Stuart to have a mean bone in his body. Yet he did. What had changed the man she once loved like an older brother? And could she get him to admit that he had been the one to strike Collin? Yet it was Stuart's excuse that made her more worried. Was he the terrible man Collin feared him to be?

She thought for certain Mrs. Thompson was involved somehow. The day of the incident, the housekeeper's gown had been soiled, and the servant appeared most perplexed when Cassandra asked her about the dress. Plus, there was the fact that the housekeeper kept mentioning plans to get Collin out of the house.

Through the reflection in the window, Cassandra noticed Collin walking closer to her. She didn't know if he still hated her for wanting to trap him into marriage or not. But she couldn't bear seeing the look of rejection in those eyes she had once become lost in. She wouldn't be able to handle hearing his blame for ruining *his* life just because his cousin had lied to her the whole time and she didn't know it. Living with this guilt was difficult enough.

"Forgive me," he said in a low voice. "I have realized I'm out of place for saying this, but...do you perhaps share Stuart's feelings?"

Gasping, she spun toward him. His face was filled with grief as he stared at her. "*Share Stuart's feelings?* You cannot be serious."

"But I am."

"Do you honestly believe I could feel that way about him, especially after all you and I have been through?"

He shrugged. "I don't know what to believe anymore. Many things have changed between us in one year, so who is to say you haven't fallen in love with Stuart?"

She stepped toward him. "I need to know something, and I want you to be honest."

"I have been nothing but honest with you, Cassandra."

Shame for what she had done to him weighed heavily on her chest. He had been honest, but after she married Lloyd, she never believed it. "Then tell me. Has this past year changed your life?"

His stare intensified, and for many silent seconds, all she could hear was the unsteady rhythm of her heartbeat, and for those undisturbed moments, all she wanted to do was stare into his intoxicating hazel eyes.

"My sweet Cass." He sighed. "Not only did your life get ruined, but my cousin's betrayal destroyed my life as well. For the first time that I can remember, I fell in love with a woman, only to have her marry someone else. I had been so in love with you, Cassandra, that I would have done anything to win your heart."

As she gazed upon this remarkable man, hope swelled in her chest. Yet she feared to let it affect her in any way. Too many horrible things had happened between them, and she would always be the one to blame.

"How can that be?" Her voice warbled.

He gave her a crooked smile. "It just happened. You are unlike any woman I have ever met, and when we got to know each other that night at the ball and then later at your home, I knew you had enchanted me."

Tears burned her eyes, but she blinked them away. She must be dreaming. His words were so unreal. "No, I mean"—she inhaled a shaky breath—"that after blaming you for a year, and then embarrassing you in front of your friends and family at your brother's wedding, I'm surprised that you don't loathe my very presence."

Sighing, he shook his head. "I don't care what other people think of me. If I did, I wouldn't have ridden after you when you left Adrian's party." He stepped closer. "Cassandra, all I wanted was to talk to you alone and find out what I had done to make you hate me. I didn't know why you wanted to marry my cousin and not me."

She hitched a breath. "I did want to marry you, remember? That was why I tried to trap you."

He chuckled. "Yes, I remember. But I didn't know that a few days ago." He took her hand and caressed her knuckles. "My sweet Cass? Will you forgive me for not stopping your wedding?"

Her body trembled as she nodded. "As long as you will forgive me for believing your cousin." She tried to gain composure, but his hazel stare made her weak in the worst way, and the guilt she had experienced was slowly fading. "Collin, you had my heart a year ago. That was what made everything so awful when my father forced me to marry your cousin. And that was why on my wedding day, I prayed you would come stop me from entering into a loveless marriage."

A sparkle lit his eyes as he lifted her hand to his mouth and kissed her knuckles. "Oh, my sweet Cass. Why were we forced to live without each other this past year, we will never know. But I want to move forward with our lives and make things better. I want…"

He paused, and as she waited for him to continue, her heart-beat raced. She didn't dare add words to finish his sentence, but she hoped they would be the words she had waited so long to hear. "You want…" she encouraged him.

He pulled her closer as he placed her palms on his chest. "My dearest Cassandra, you would make me a very happy man if you agreed—"

Suddenly, the door flew open and smacked against the wall. Both Cassandra and Collin jumped. Stuart stood at the open doorway holding a pistol, pointing it at Collin.

"Stuart, no!" Cassandra gasped.

Collin stepped in front of her, blocking her from the madman holding the gun.

"You don't want to do that, Stuart," Collin said slowly.

"Oh, believe me…this is what I have wanted to do for quite a while. I need to protect Cassandra from men like you." Stuart glared at Collin. "That was why I convinced Lord Kentwood that she was only after you for your money. And that was why I wrote the note and signed your name." He released an evil laugh. "It was easy to convince the drunken lord that you were planning on meeting Miss Featherstone at the abandoned cottage, and being a true friend, he set out to stop you from falling into the trap."

Cassandra's chest tightened and tears blurred her vision. Stuart had done that? Why would he? It couldn't be because he thought he loved her.

Collin cussed and lunged for Stuart, but the servant had been prepared, and jumped back. His gaze narrowed on Collin as he shook his head.

"You best be careful, my lord, or your fate will be the same as your poor, drunken cousin."

Confusion filled her, but her mind opened. He couldn't pos-sibly… No, she refused to believe it. "Stuart? What in the blazes are you talking about? Lloyd drowned. Why would you think that Collin would have the same fate?"

Stuart arched a bushy eyebrow. "Forgive me for not making myself clear," he said. "What I meant to say was that I would dispose of the new Lord Kentwood just as easily as I disposed of his cousin."

Cassandra's gasp matched Collin's. She swayed, but quickly righted herself. "No, Stuart. Why?" Her voice broke.

"Because he loves you," Collin answered.

Stuart shrugged, wearing a smug expression. "Yes, I love her, but it is more than that. You see, I was a little boy when my father worked for the first Lord Kentwood. The lord had no sons, and promised my father that someday the estate would fall into my hands."

Collin snorted. "That is impossible. The lands are handed to the next in line to inherit."

Stuart threw him a glare. "You think I don't know that? But then, when I was ten years old, the lord's mistress gave birth to a boy—Lloyd."

Cassandra sucked in another breath. "He was illegitimate?"

Nodding, Stuart scrubbed a hand over his chin. "Indeed, but the first Lord Kentwood was so happy to finally have a child that he made everyone believe Lloyd was legitimate."

Collin folded his arms. "Let me finish this story for you. Now that the lord had a son, you were no longer in the running to get the estate. So then when you saw the opportunity to get closer to Lloyd by causing him and Cassandra to get caught, you controlled every step of the way, hoping that one day Cassandra would fall in love with you and allow you to *think* the estate was yours."

Stuart nodded sharply. "You are more intelligent than I gave you credit for."

"However, you have overlooked one thing," Collin continued. "You do not have noble blood, and therefore, you will *never* have an estate of your own. Cassandra, being a widow, would have had to live wherever the current Lord Kentwood assigned her to live."

Stuart's glare turned darker as his steady hand raised the pistol toward Collin. "And I would kill you, too."

Collin shook his head. "What about the next one to inherit the title? That would be my brother, Adrian."

"You don't know me, *my lord*. I will do anything to take over *my* estate. This place should have been mine."

Bitterness coated Cassandra's tongue as bile rose in her throat. Stuart had completely lost his mind. No matter what Collin said, he would never be able to convince Stuart otherwise.

Glancing around, she searched for something that might be used to stop Stuart, or at least distract him so that Collin could get the pistol. Unfortunately, there wasn't anything she could use as a weapon. There was only one thing she could do to stop him. Stuart had always seemed to know her thoughts and feelings. She prayed this time he wouldn't be able to suspect that she was playacting.

"Indeed it should." She slowly moved past Collin. His arm shot out to hold her back, but she gently pushed it away, keeping her focus on Stuart. "What the first Lord Kentwood did to you was unforgivable." She tried to keep her voice sweet, even though disappointment for her family's friend was breaking her heart. Thankfully, Stuart allowed her to stand beside him and touch his arm.

"Yes, but do you know what will even be worse?" he asked.

"What?" She tried staring at him as though she loved him.

"If you fall for *his* false charms." Stuart shook his head. "He doesn't love you like I do, Cassandra."

She heard Collin's angry breaths behind her, but she couldn't look back at him. By peering into Collin's eyes, Stuart would be able to know how much she loved him. So, for now, she must not lose eye contact with Stuart.

"You have always been there for me, you know. I wouldn't have been able to make it through this year of mourning without your working beside me and showing me the respect those other servants failed to give me."

Gradually, the arm holding the pistol lowered. "I have, and I always will. You can always count on me."

"That is the kind of man I want to call my husband. That is the kind of man I want sharing my life."

Stuart's expression relaxed. "Then look no further. I'm right here."

A loud growl rent the air, followed by Collin's fist flying toward Stuart. Before he could do anything, Collin hit him in the nose. The sound of breaking bones echoed in the room. Seconds later, Stuart crumpled to the ground. In a flash, Collin snatched the pistol out of the man's grasp.

"She has already found that man, you imbecile," he snapped, glowering at Stuart, who held his bloody nose. "Did you honestly think you could make her a good husband if you killed others who got in your way? Because if you think that way, then your mind is too far gone to save it."

The door to the parlor opened again. This time it was Mrs. Thompson who entered. Her gaze dropped to Stuart on the floor, and she slapped a hand over her mouth and shook her head. Tears gathered in her eyes.

"Dora?" Cassandra asked. "Did you know Stuart was the one who attacked Lord Kentwood?"

The woman met Cassandra's gaze. The housekeeper didn't have to say a word, because guilt was all over her expression.

"Dora?" Cassandra asked again, trying to keep her voice calm. "Did you help Stuart in any way?"

"N-no, my lady. I saw him running away that morning, and I assumed he was the culprit. But I also thought he did it to try to keep Lord Kentwood away." She sniffed and rubbed her sleeve under her nose. "None of us wanted him here, and, well, since Stuart was your family friend, I thought that was why he hit the nobleman."

Cassandra took a shaky breath. "Mrs. Thompson, will you send one of the other maids in here, please? Also, send Riddle and Bentley as well."

"Yes, my lady."

As soon the housekeeper left, Collin wrapped both arms around her, pulling her against his chest. Sighing, she leaned next to him and closed her eyes. Warmth surrounded her, just as it had always done when Collin held her.

"Why did you call for those other servants?" he asked.

"I will send my driver to fetch the constable, and the footman to take this miserable excuse for a man"—she pointed toward Stuart on the floor, holding his bloody nose—"out of my sight."

"What a wonderful plan." Collin smiled and kissed her forehead.

"Oh, Collin. I was so scared."

He stroked her cheek. "I lost you once, but I don't plan on making that mistake again."

She looked up. When their gazes met, his face relaxed and he smiled.

"I thank you for distracting him." He winked. "We work well together, don't you think?"

Happiness filled her, and she smiled, resting both palms on his strong chest. "I have always thought that, my love."

"Then what do you say we make this a permanent arrangement?"

Nodding, she sighed. "There is nothing in this world that I want more, except maybe to get my *former* butler arrested for murder and for ruining people's lives and having my *former* housekeeper arrested as an accomplice."

"Don't worry, my sweet Cass. Your wish is my command."

Epilogue

COLLIN CUDDLED ON the sofa with his new wife, enjoying their privacy now that the wedding crowd had left. The low-burning fire made their surroundings more peaceful.

Although he had wanted to give her a large wedding—since Lloyd had never given her that—instead, she asked for a smaller wedding with just a few friends and their families. She also wanted the opportunity to apologize to Adrian and Bridget for arriving uninvited at their wedding and causing a dreadful scene. Thankfully, Collin's younger brother and new wife were very understanding, and welcomed Cassandra into the family with open arms.

Rubbing her cheek on his chest, she sighed heavily. "I thought this day would never arrive."

"I agree. It has been a very strenuous two weeks." He plucked the pins holding her hair in a bun, releasing them to allow her glorious hair to fall around her shoulders and down her back.

"I'm very grateful your family was so nice to me."

He cupped her chin and tilted her head back until her attention was on his eyes. "My darling wife, they know how unhappy I have been since you wed Lloyd. They know you are the reason there are stars in my eyes and love in my heart now."

"Oh, Collin." She caressed his chest. "Will you ever forgive me for the things I said to you out of anger?"

"They are forgotten, my love." He gently brushed his lips over hers. When he pulled away, her expression was filled with desire. "Are you ready to go upstairs?" His voice was low as seduction filled his mind.

She grinned. "I thought you would never ask, but…" Her face reddened. "You must know something first."

"What is it, my sweet Cass?"

"I'm still a…" She swallowed hard. "You see, I was never…" She cleared her throat. "Lloyd never touched me. Not when we were caught in the cottage, and especially not on our wedding night. He passed out drunk right after we had reached the manor."

Collin's heart hammered with excitement. Knowing he would be her first made him happier any man should be.

He took a deep breath, trying to control the desire rushing through him. "I'm so very relieved to hear that, but I would love you regardless."

"I know." She caressed his cheek. "But I wanted to make certain there were no surprises on our wedding night."

Gathering her close, he kissed her again, deepening it this time. She wrapped her arms around his neck and responded eagerly. He moved to the buttons on the back of her dress, and unfastened them one by one. Making love to her would always be foremost on his mind, especially because he knew how passionate she was.

She broke the kiss and pulled back. Her eyes were wide with curiosity. "Collin, what are you doing? Should we not be doing *that* upstairs?"

He chuckled. "My love, the wonderful thing about being married and in love is that we can do this anywhere—and at any time—we like."

Her grin widened. "Then let us not wait a moment longer."

She pushed herself against him, picking up on the kiss where they had left off. Love burst inside his chest. They were going to be so very happy together. He never thought he would be this happy, and tonight—and for the rest of their lives—he would devote himself to making her glad she had chosen to love him and none other.

Although their relationship had come together under deceptive circumstances, they were meant to be together, forever.

THE END

READERS—find more stories about the Worthington men here – authormariehiggins.com/sons-of-worthington

Join my newsletter – authormariehiggins.com/newsletter

To find more of Marie Higgins' books, click this link – authormariehiggins.com

About the Author

Marie Higgins is an award-winning, best-selling author of clean romance novels that melt your heart and have you falling in love over and over again. Since 2010, she's published over 100 heartwarming, on-the-edge-of-your-seat romances. She has broadened her readership by writing mystery/suspense, humor, time travel, and paranormal, along with her love for historical romances. Her readers have dubbed her "Queen of Tease" because of all her twists and unexpected endings.

Website – www.authormariehiggins.com
Facebook – facebook.com/marie.higgins.7543
TikTok – tiktok.com/@author.mariehiggins
Instagram – instagram.com/author.mariehiggins
Bookbub – bookbub.com/authors/marie-higgins

www.ingramcontent.com/pod-product-compliance
Lightning Source LLC
Chambersburg PA
CBHW070342010826
48976CB00017B/1143